SILLY LILLY

IN WHAT WILL I BE TODAY?

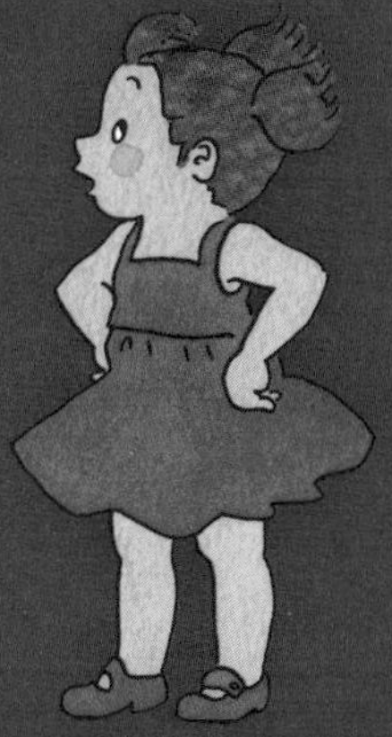

Agnès Rosenstiehl

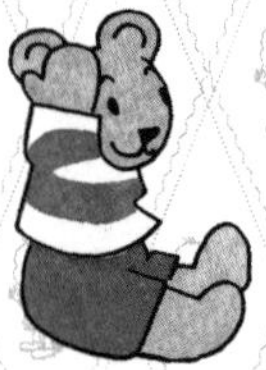

SILLY LILLY

IN WHAT WILL I BE TODAY?

A TOON BOOK BY

Agnès Rosenstiehl

TOON BOOKS IS A DIVISION OF RAW JUNIOR, LLC, NEW YORK

For Ella Choudhury

Editorial Director: FRANÇOISE MOULY

Book Design: FRANÇOISE MOULY & JONATHAN BENNETT

AGNÈS ROSENSTIEHL'S artwork was drown in india ink & watercolor

Library of Congress Cataloging-in-Publication Data:

Rosenstiehl, Agnès.

Silly Lilly in what will I be today? / by Agnès Rosenthiehl.

p. cm.

"A Toon Book."

Summary: Silly Lilly tries out a new job every day of the week, from acrobat to vampire.

ISBN 978-1-935179-08-5 (1-935179-08-x)

[1. Occupations–Fiction. 2. Cartoons and comics.] I. Title.

PZ7.R71942Sil 2010

[E]–dc22

2010005308

ISBN 13: 978-1-935179-08-5 ISBN 10: 1-935179-08-X

10 9 8 7 6 5 4 3 2 1

www.TOON-BOOKS.com

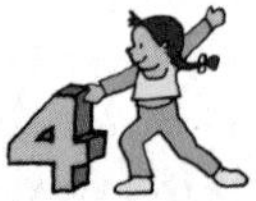

7 DAYS OF THE WEEK

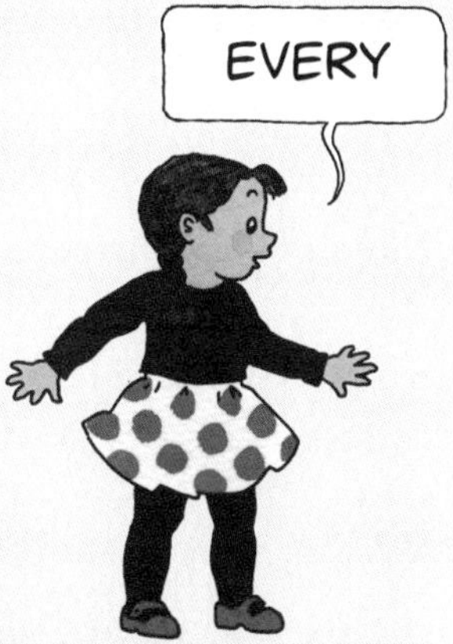
EVERY

MONDAY

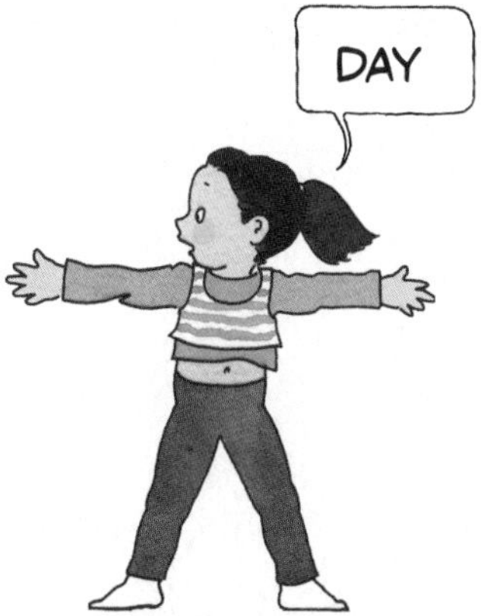
DAY

TUESDAY

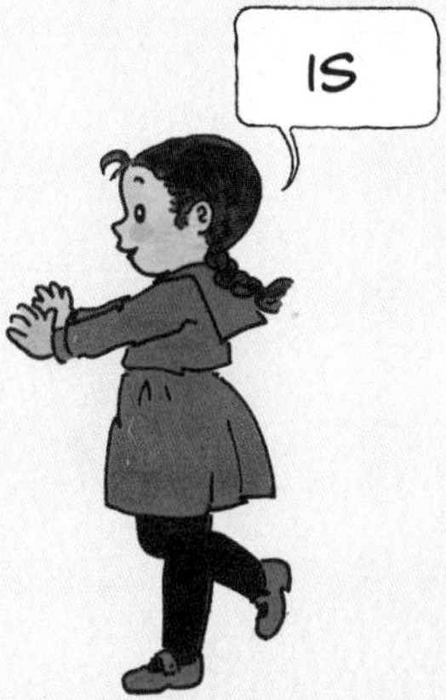
IS

WEDNESDAY

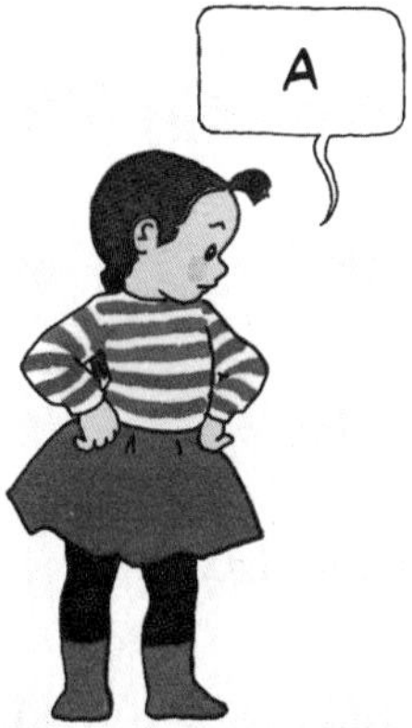
A

HURSDAY

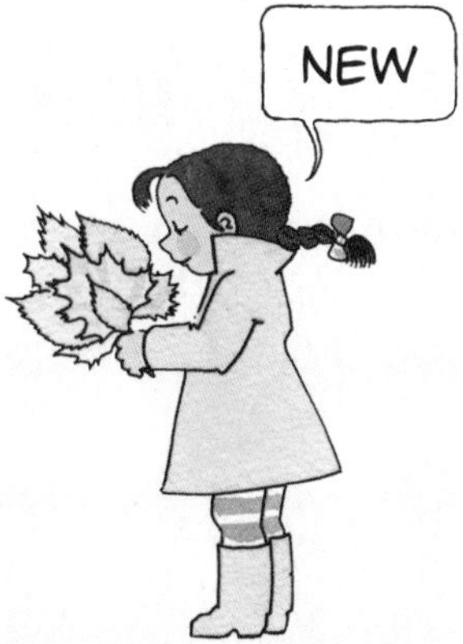
NEW

FRIDAY

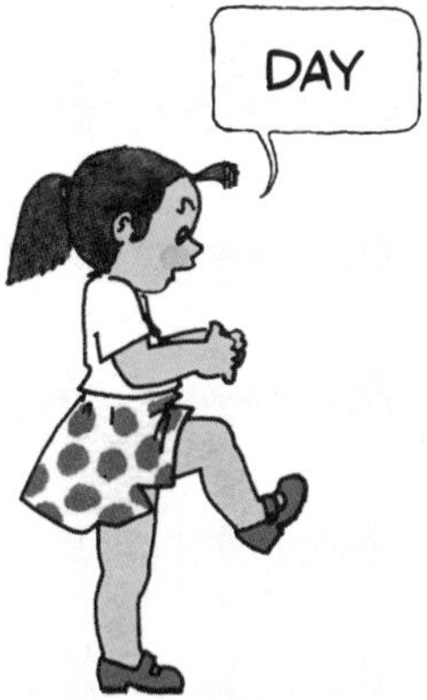
DAY

SATURDAY

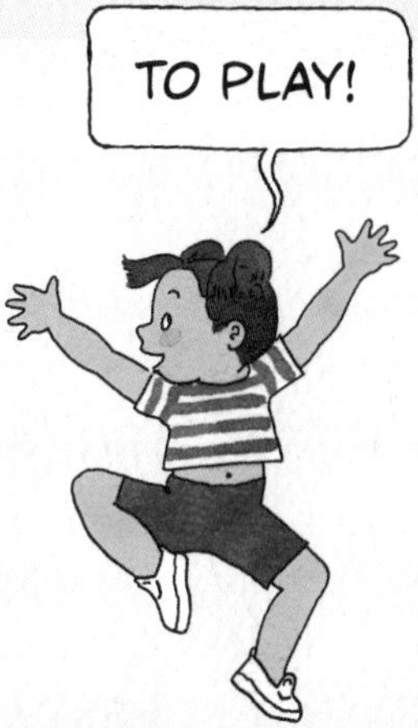
TO PLAY!

SUNDAY

SO, ON MONDAY

SILLY LILLY

IS A COOK

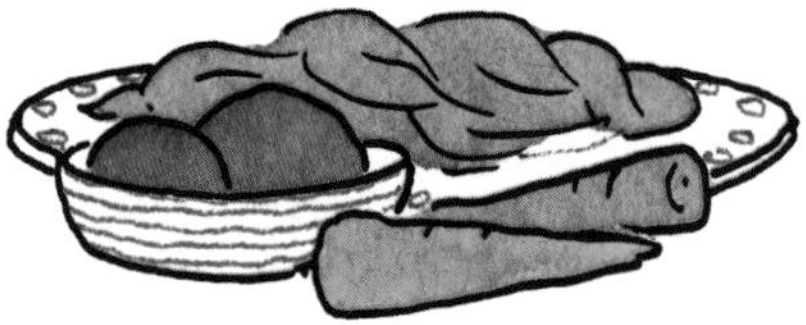

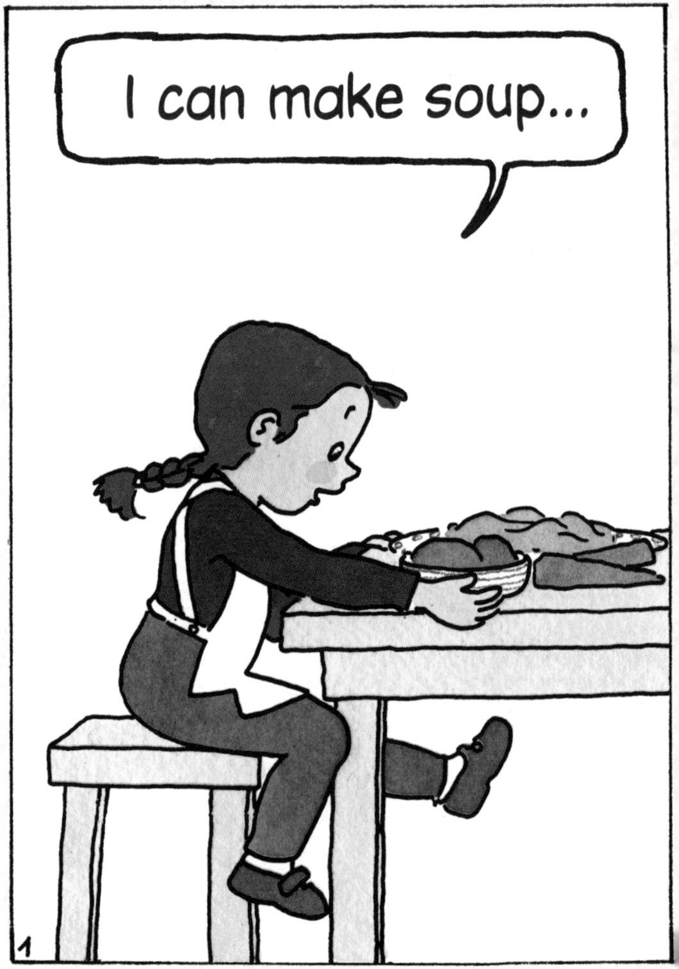
I can make soup...
1

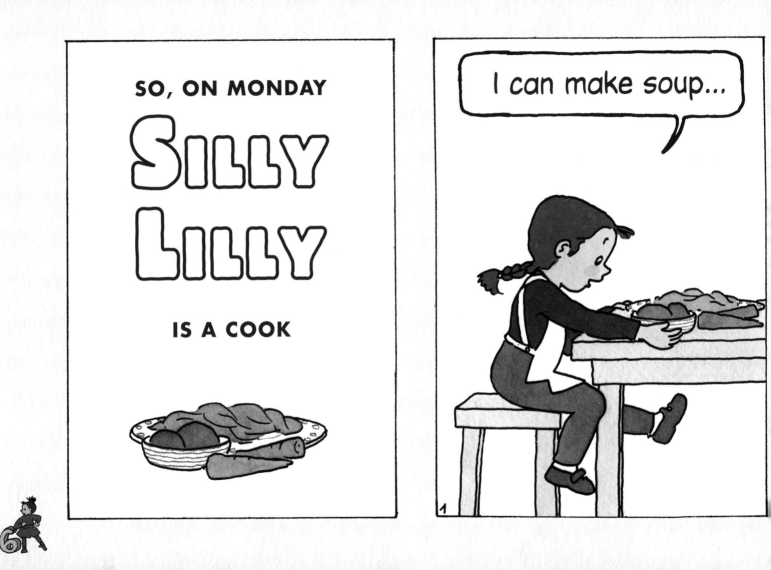

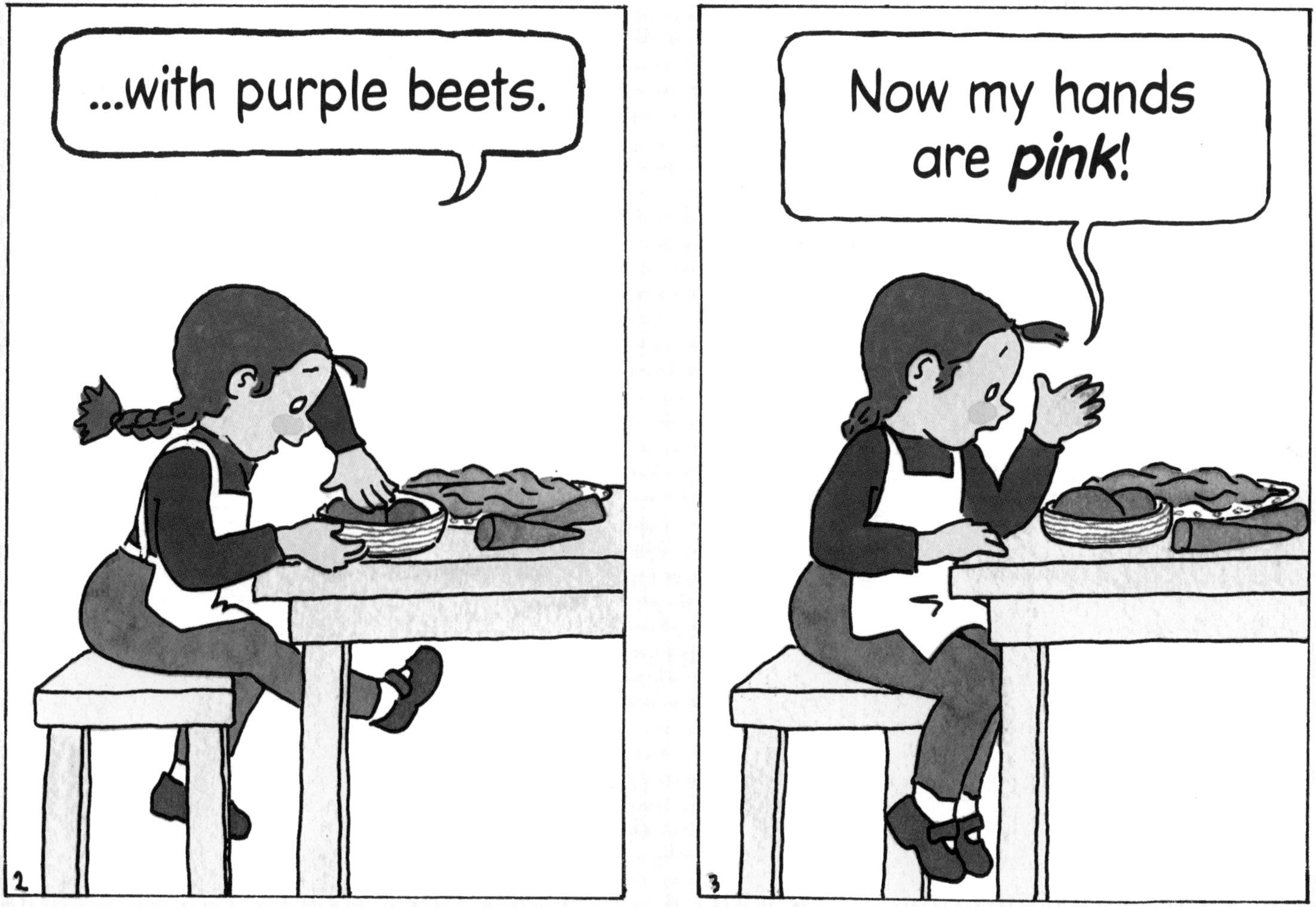
...with purple beets.
Now my hands are **pink**!

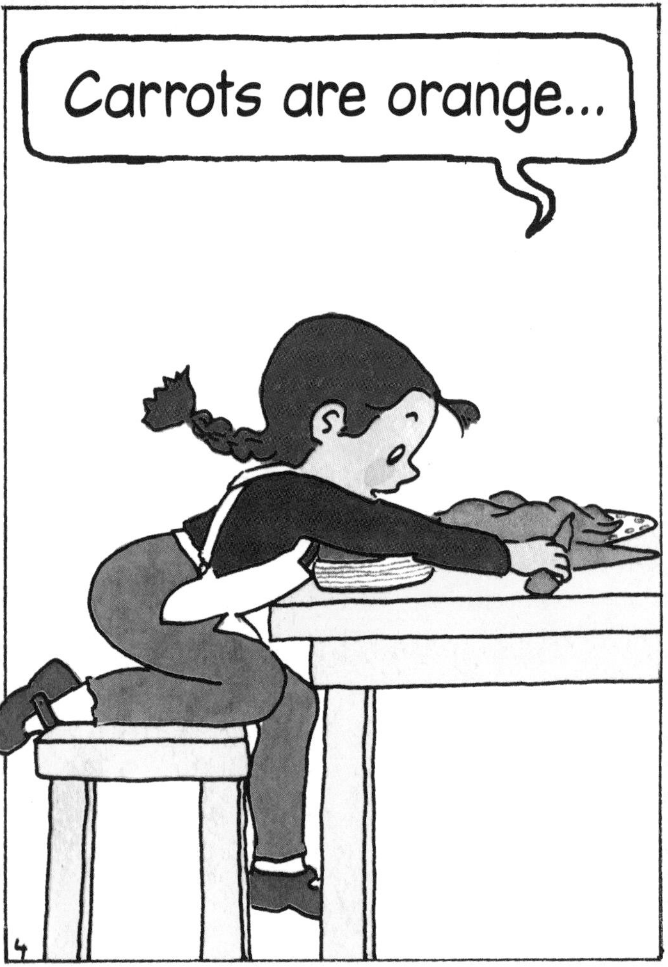
Carrots are orange...
4

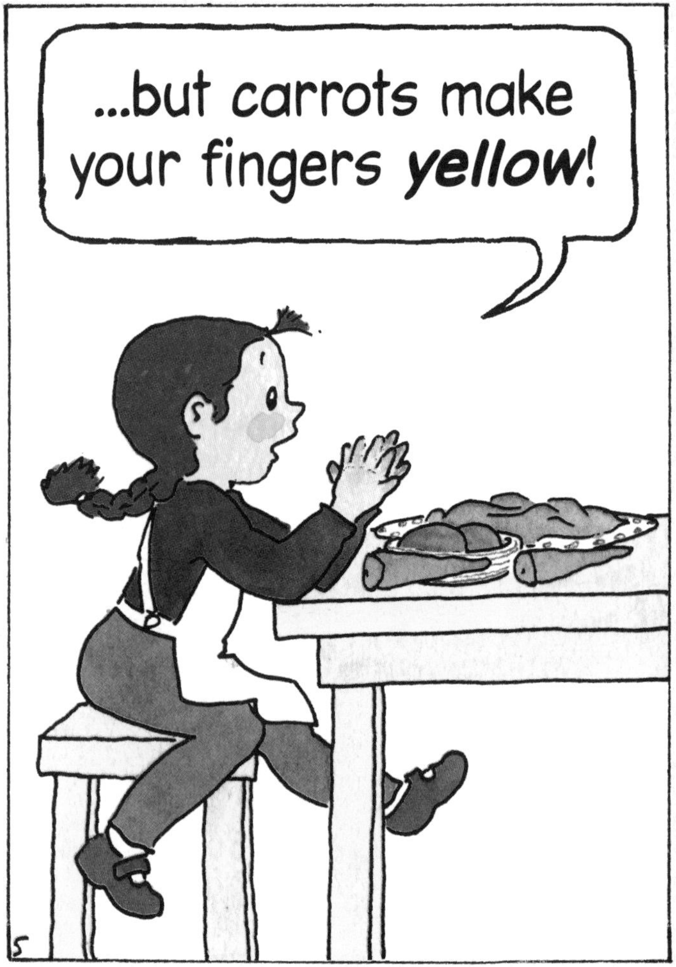
...but carrots make your fingers ***yellow***!
5

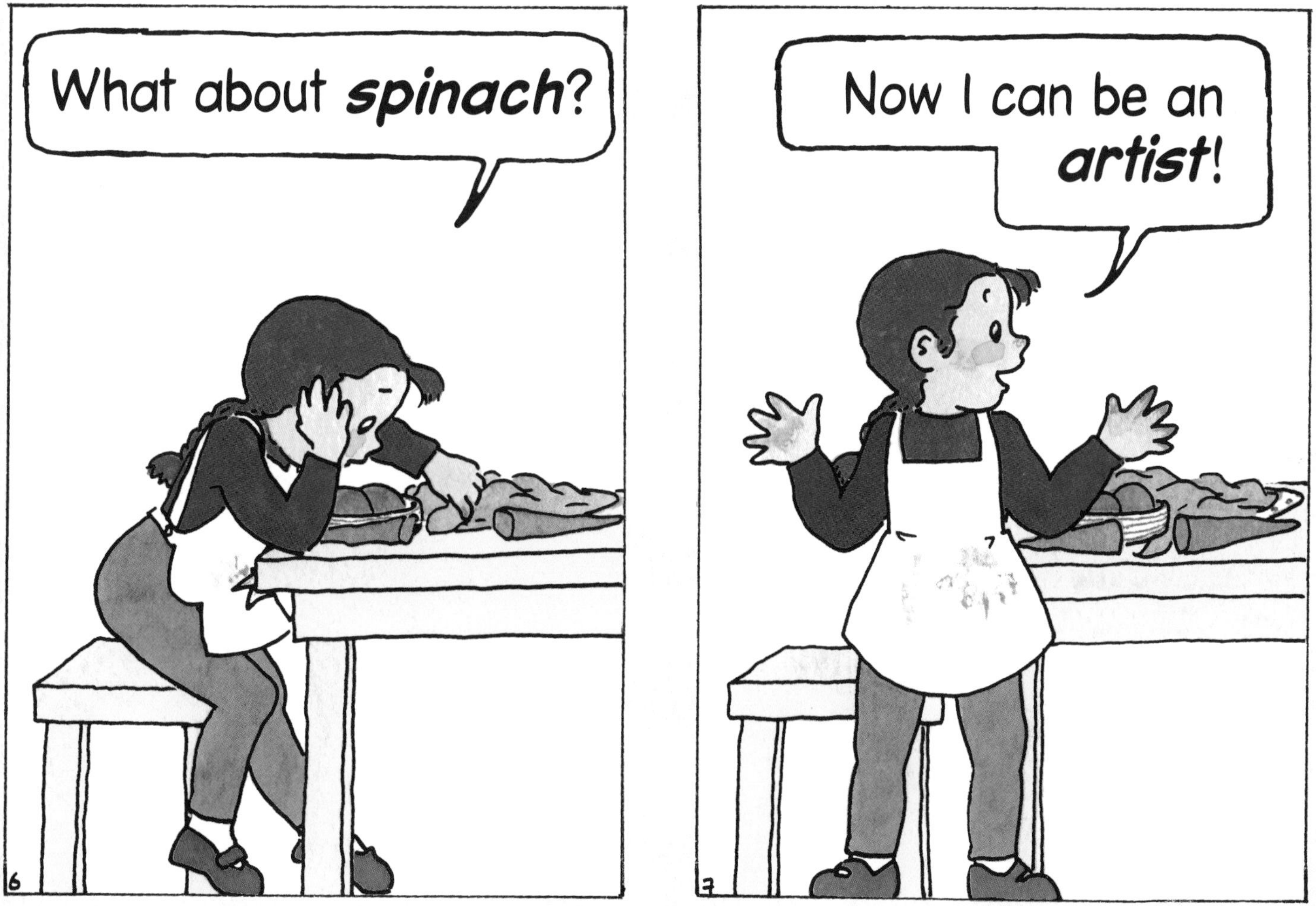
What about ***spinach***?
6
Now I can be an ***artist***!
7

SO, ON TUESDAY

SILLY LILLY

IS A CITY PLANNER

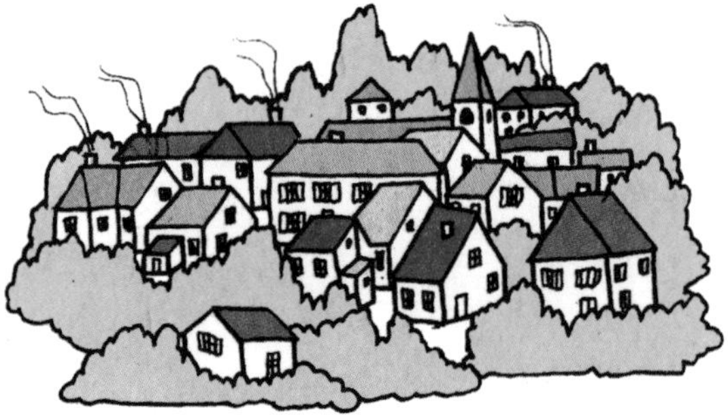

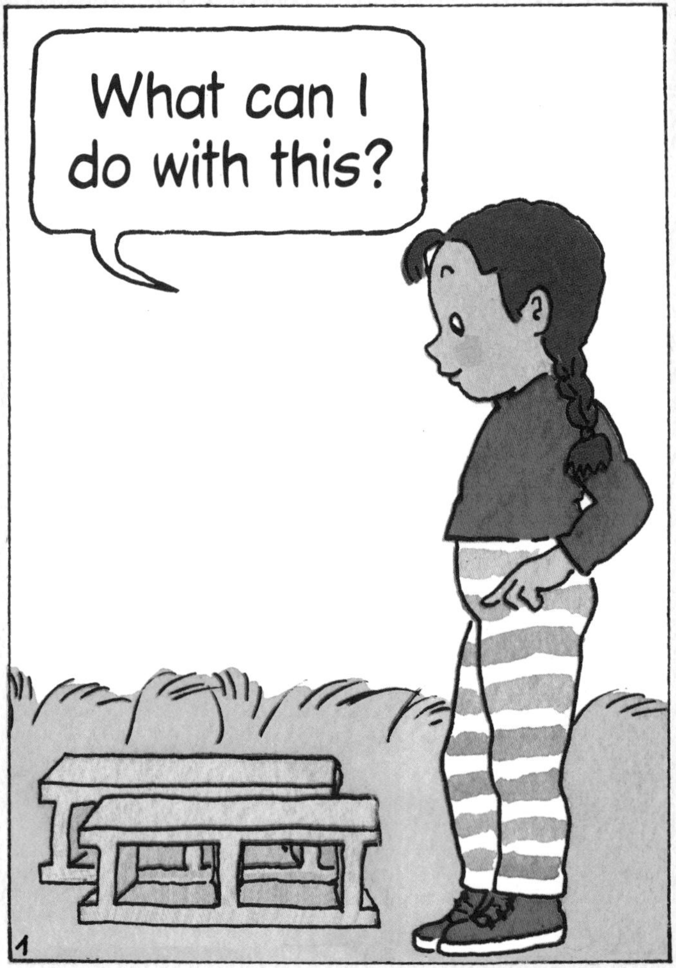
What can I do with this?
1

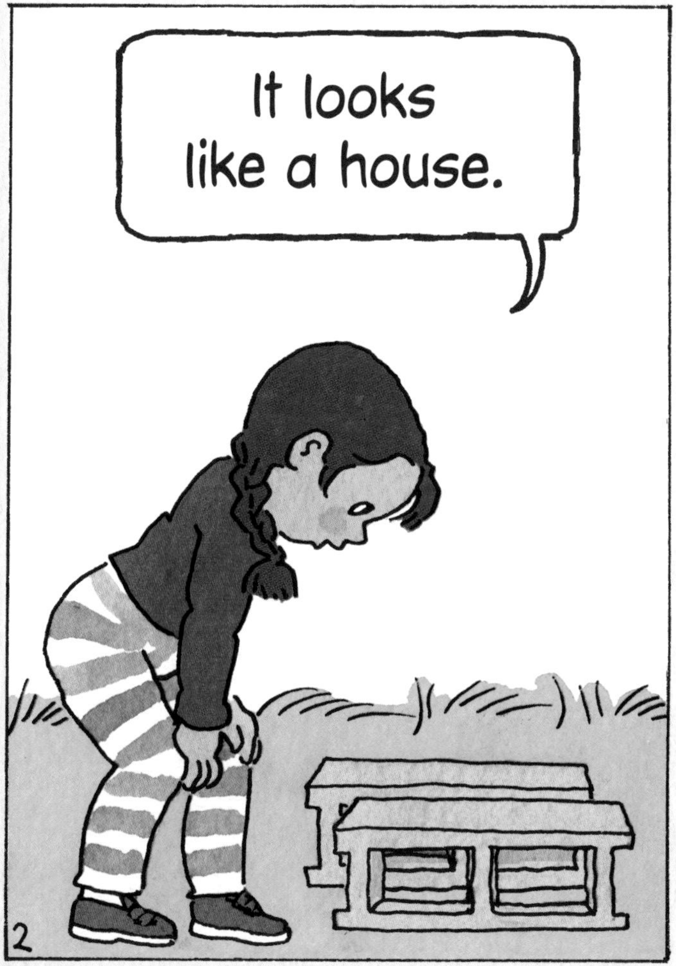
It looks like a house.
2

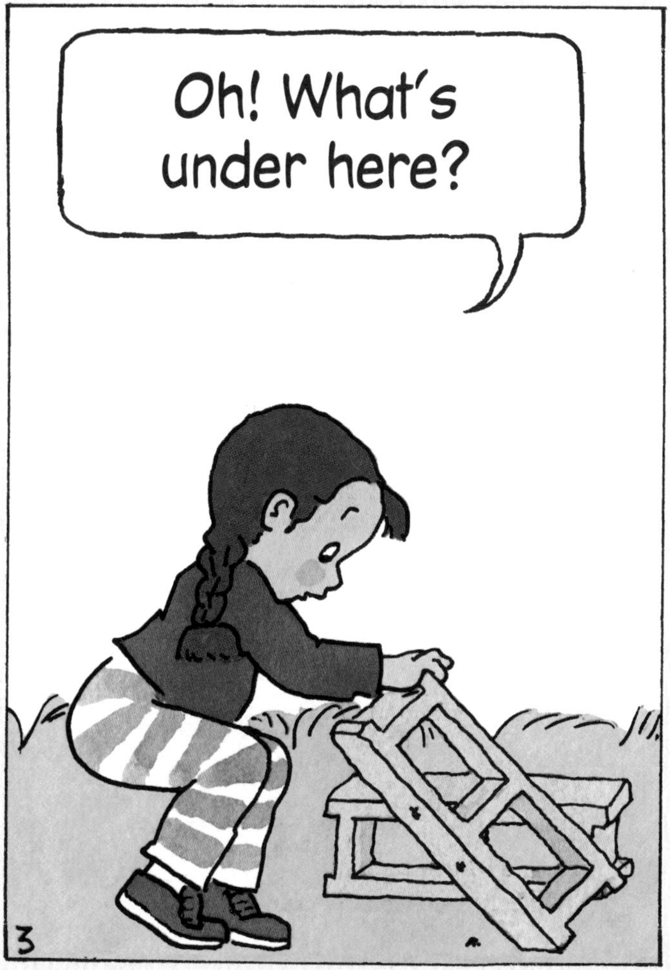
Oh! What's under here?
3

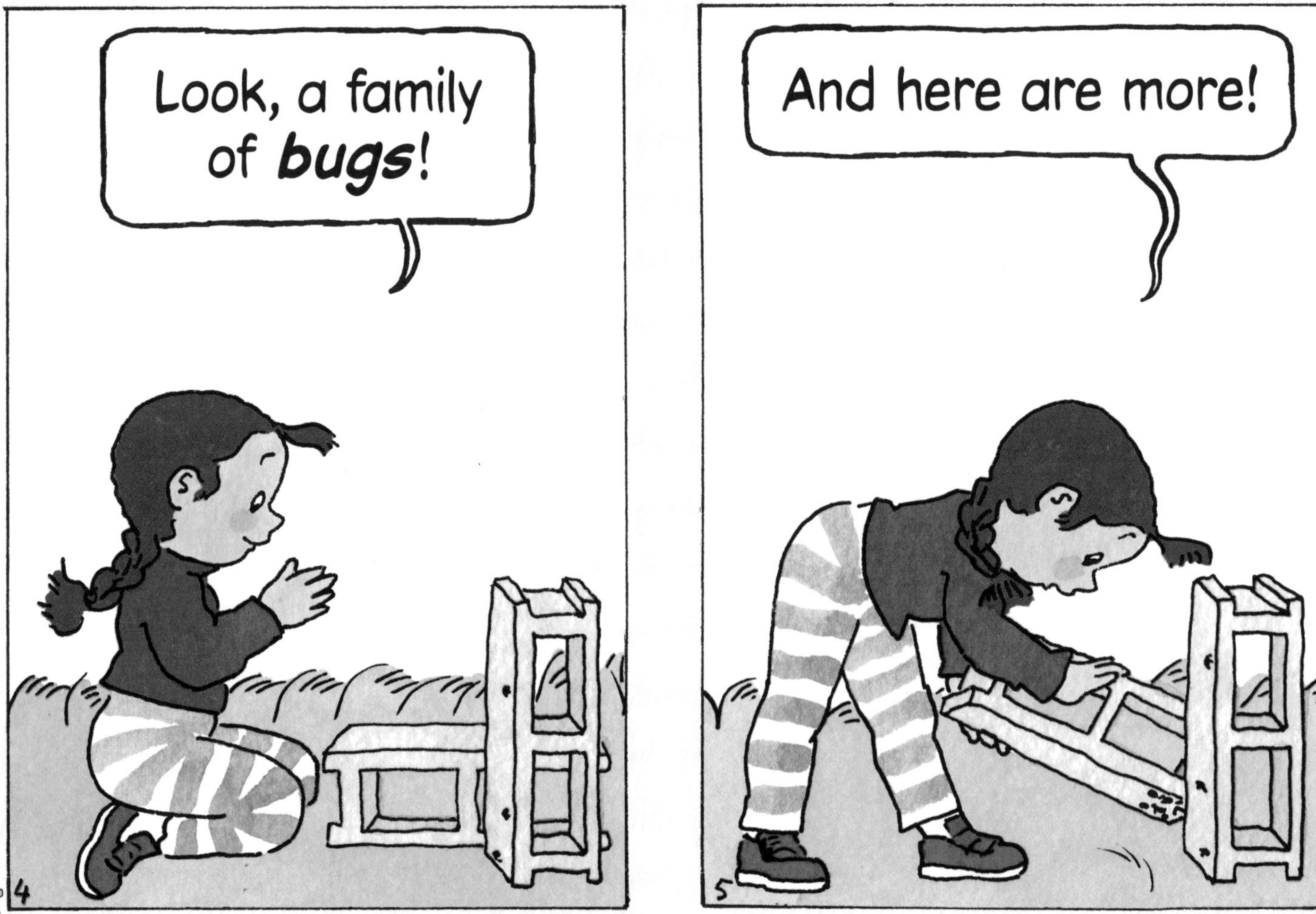
Look, a family of **bugs**!
And here are more!

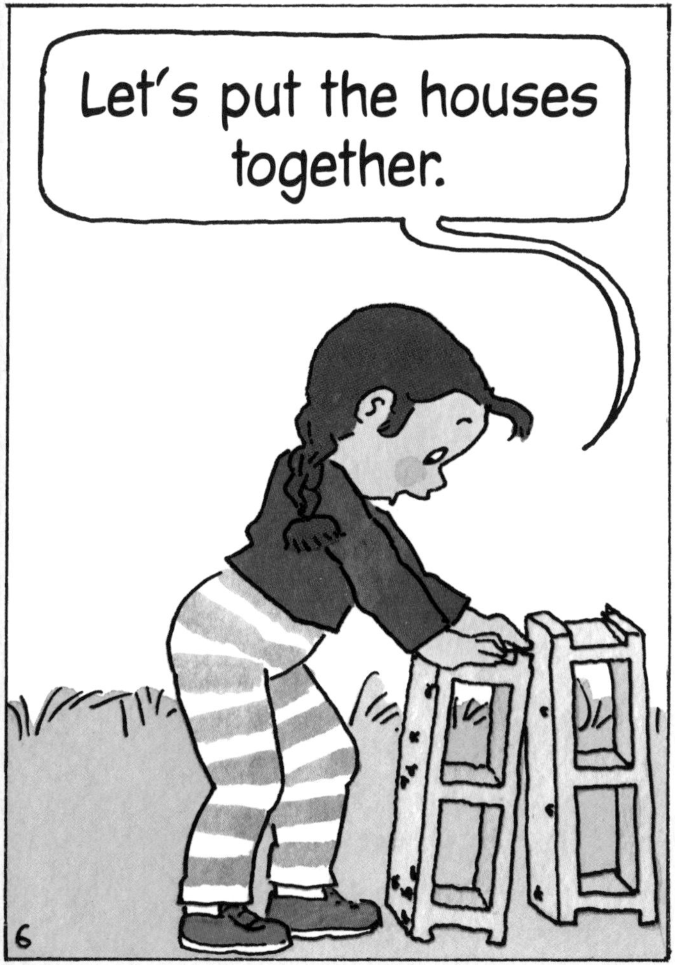
Let's put the houses together.
6

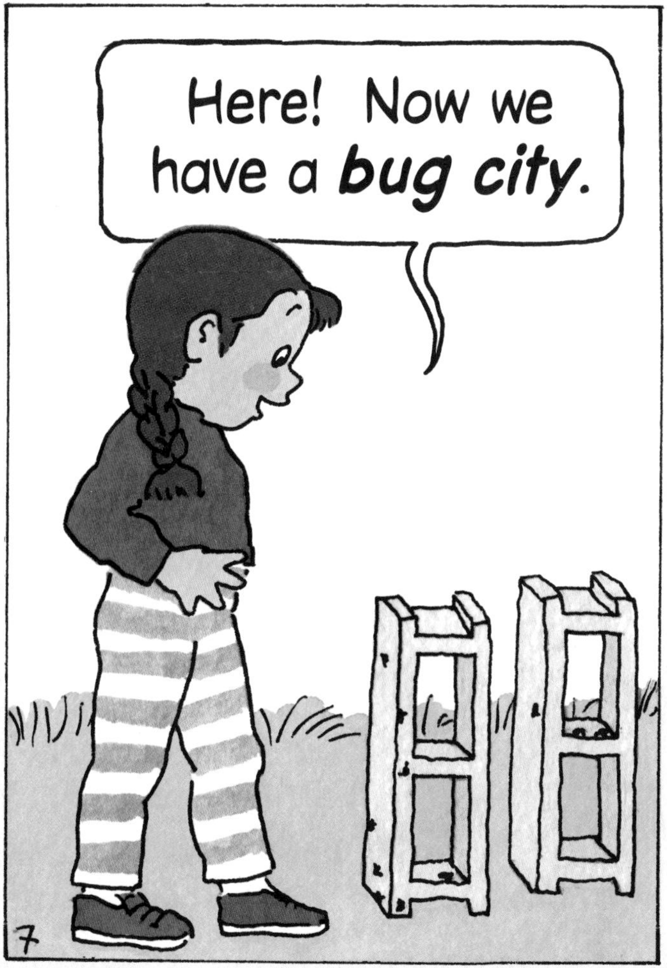
Here! Now we have a **bug city**.
7

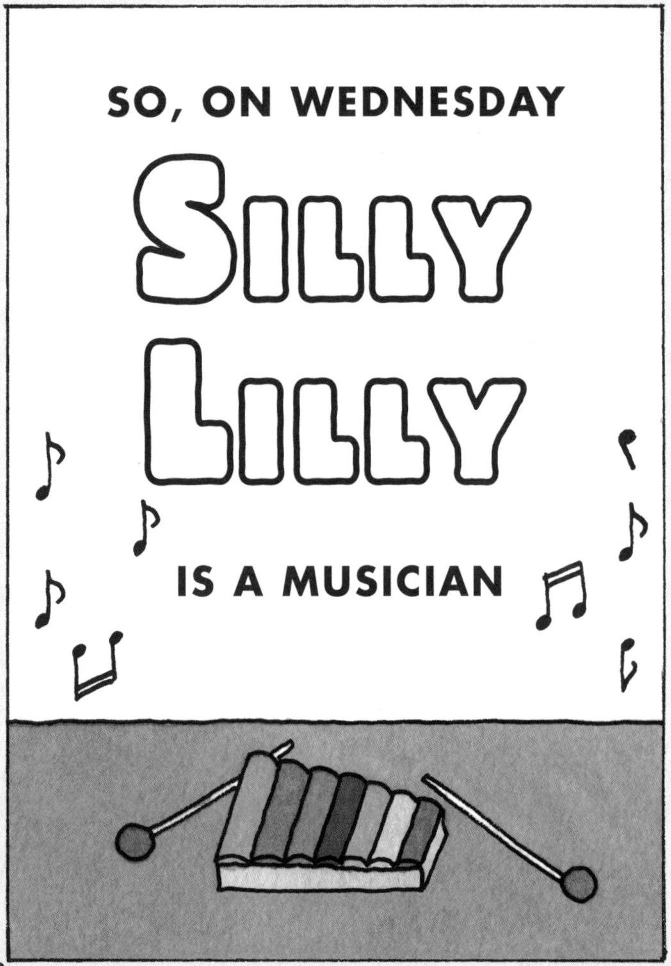
SO, ON WEDNESDAY
SILLY
LILLY
IS A MUSICIAN

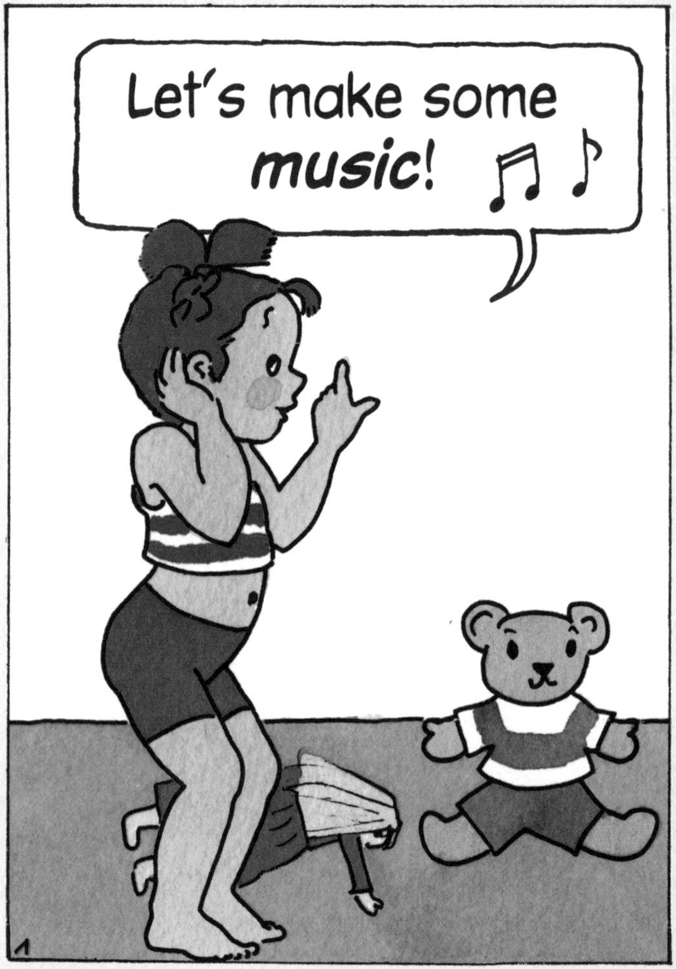
Let's make some *music*!

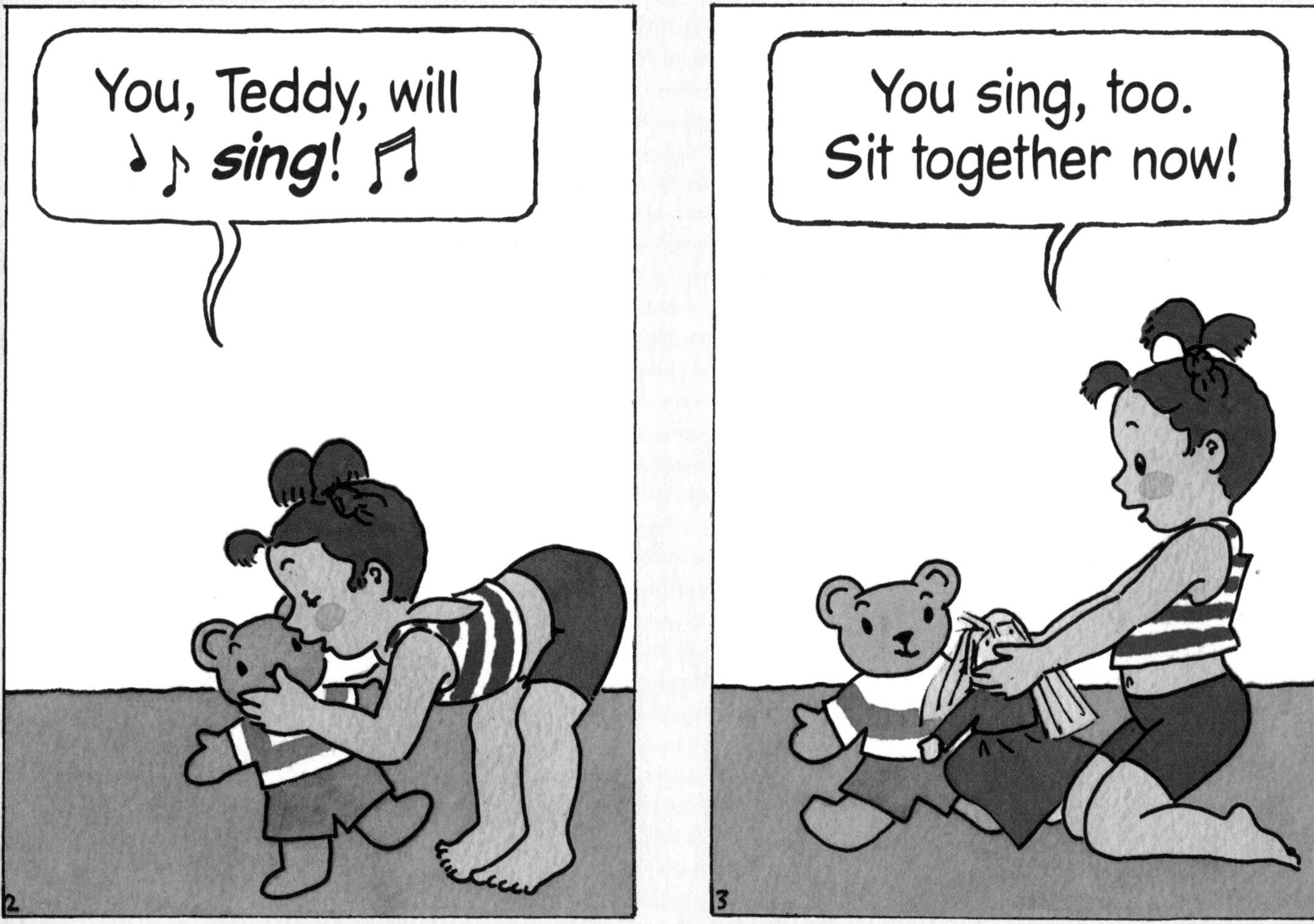
You, Teddy, will ♪ ♪ *sing*! ♫
You sing, too. Sit together now!

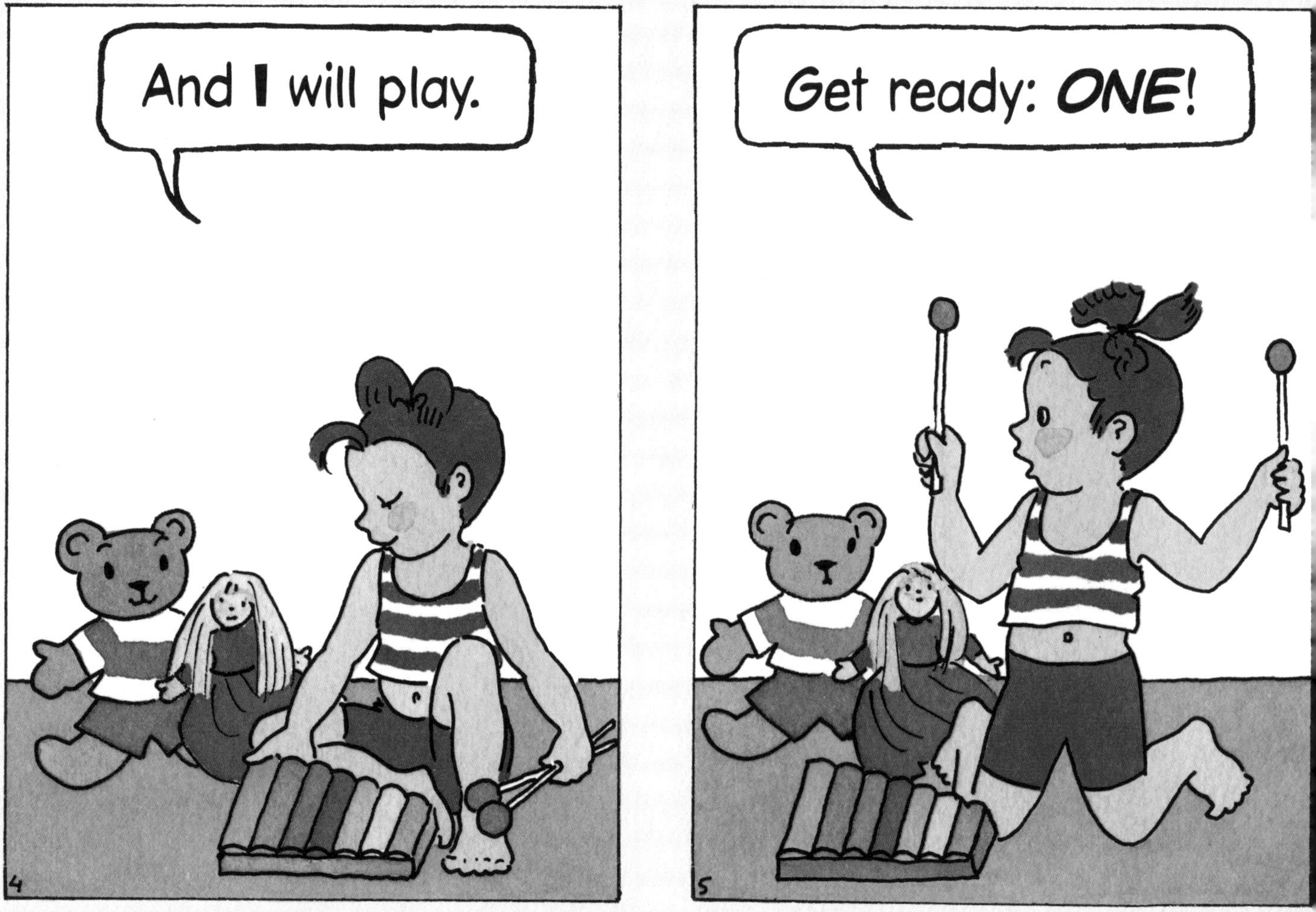
And I will play.
4
Get ready: ONE!
5

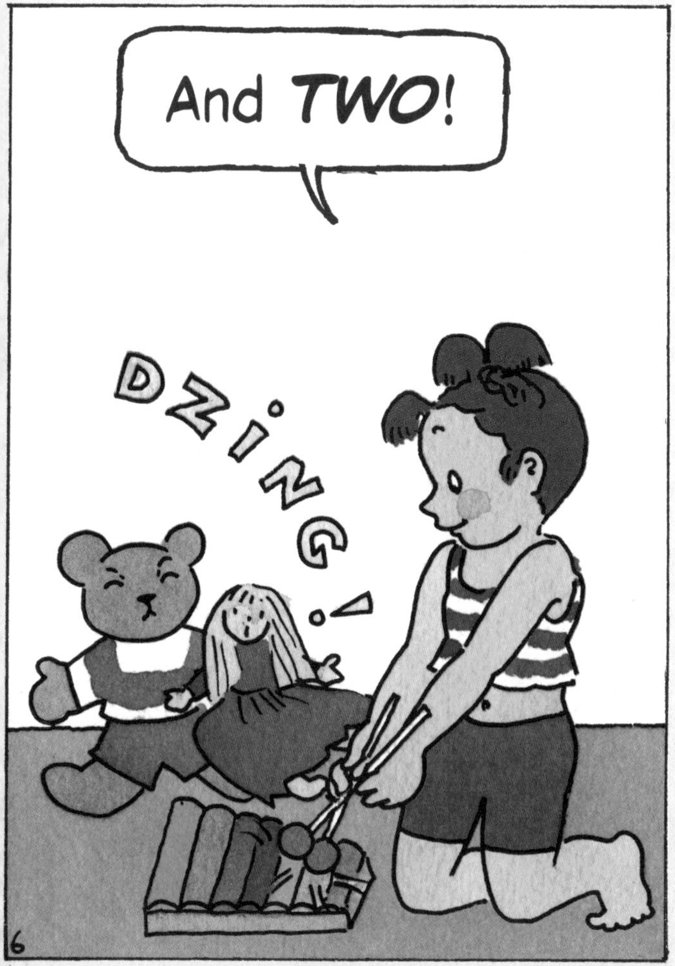
And TWO!
DZING!
6

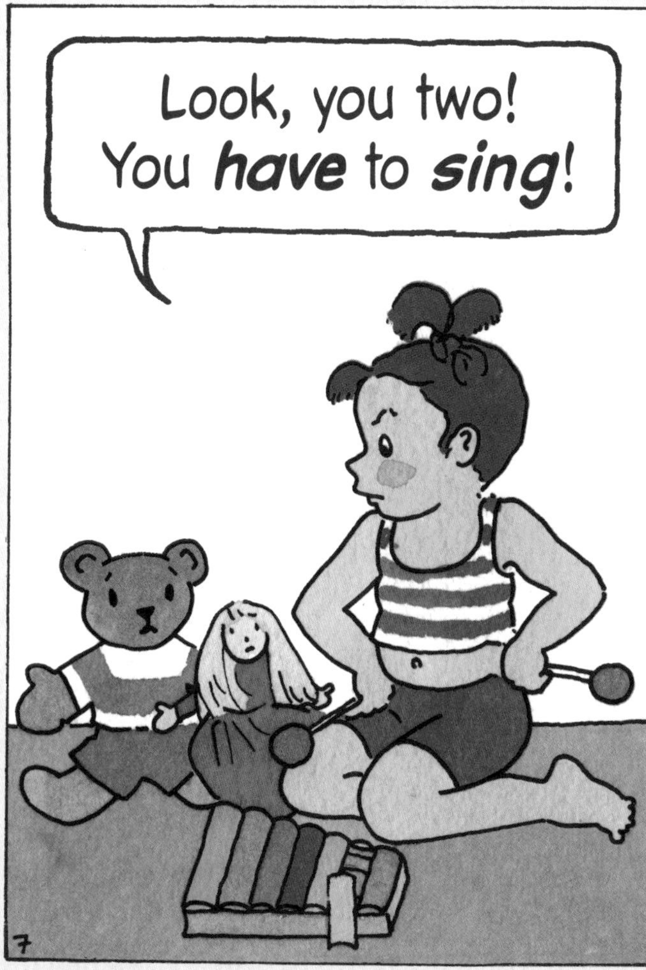
Look, you two!
You have to sing!
7

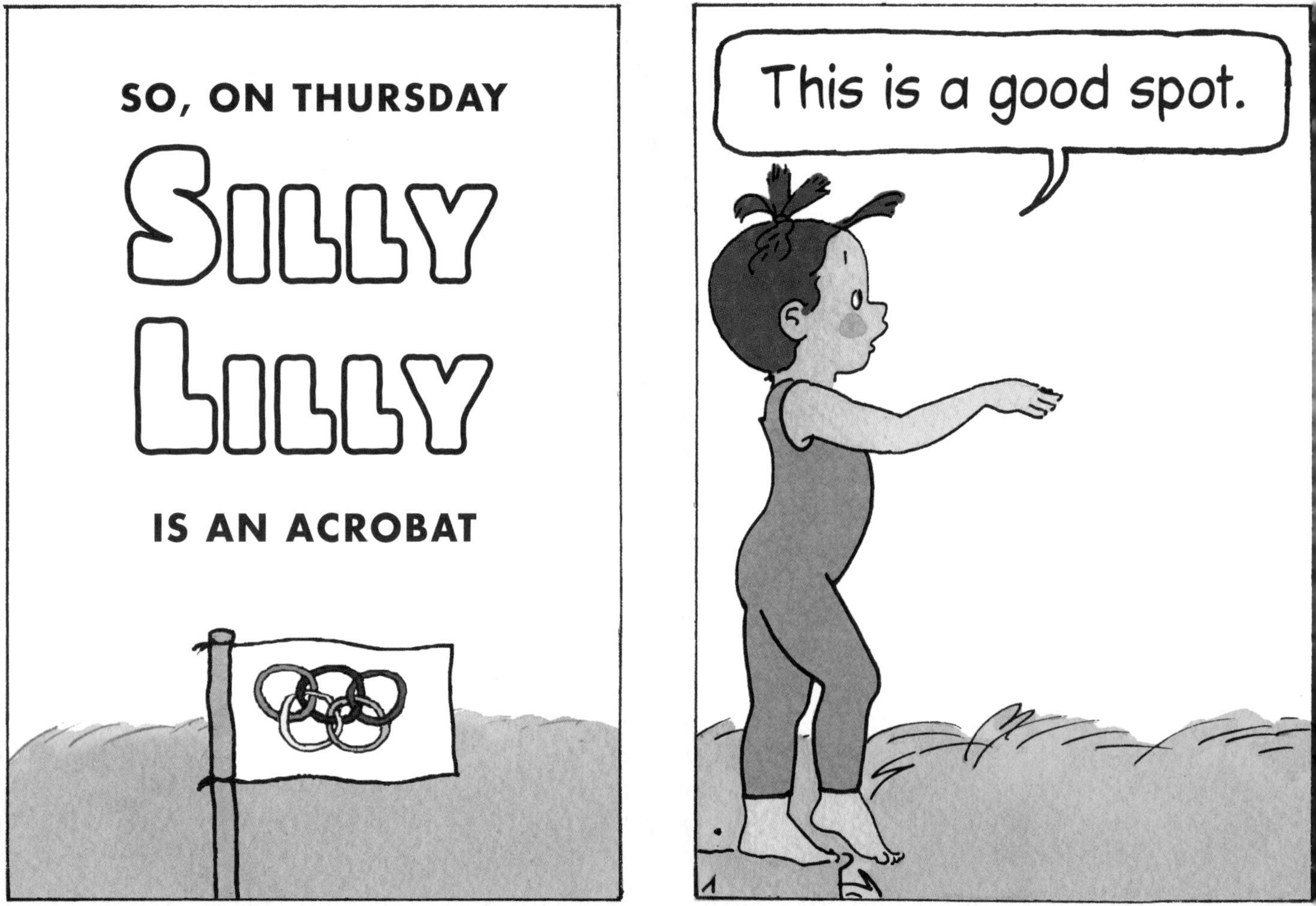
SO, ON THURSDAY
SILLY LILLY
IS AN ACROBAT
This is a good spot.

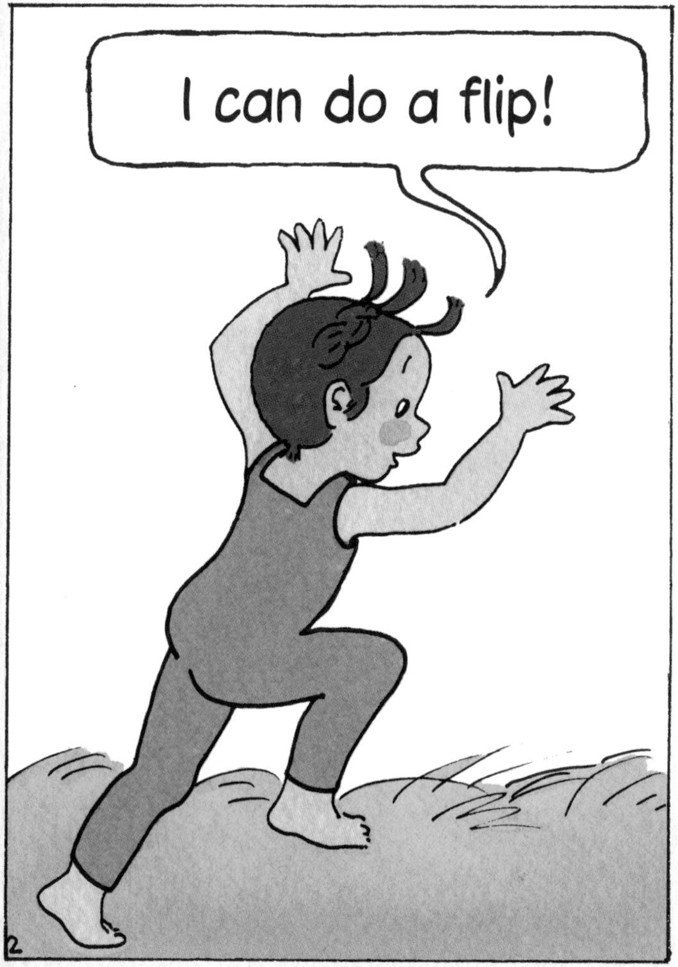
I can do a flip!
2

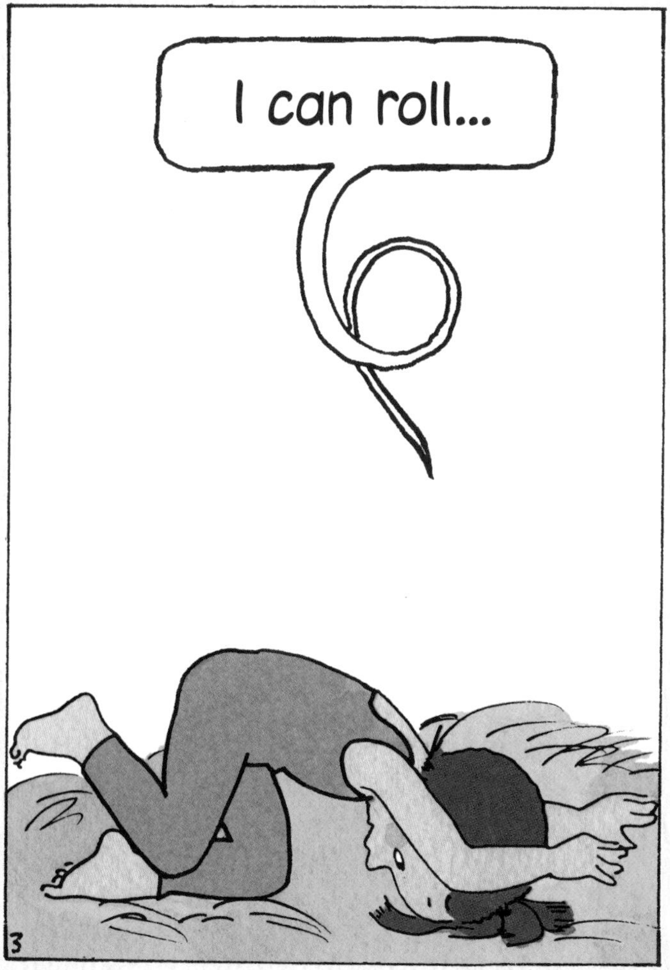
I can roll...
3

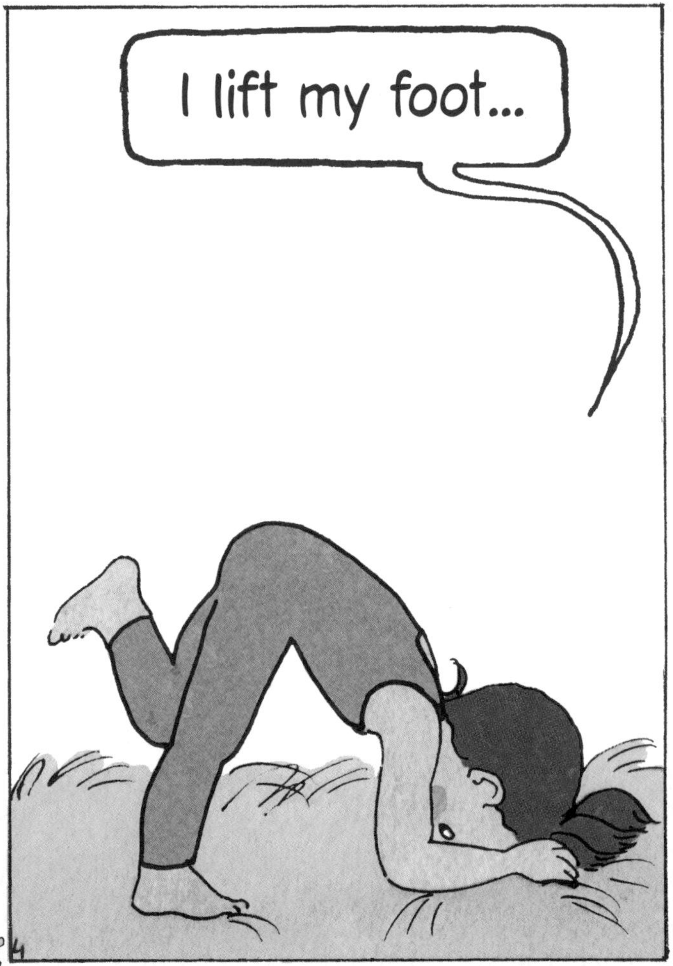
I lift my foot...
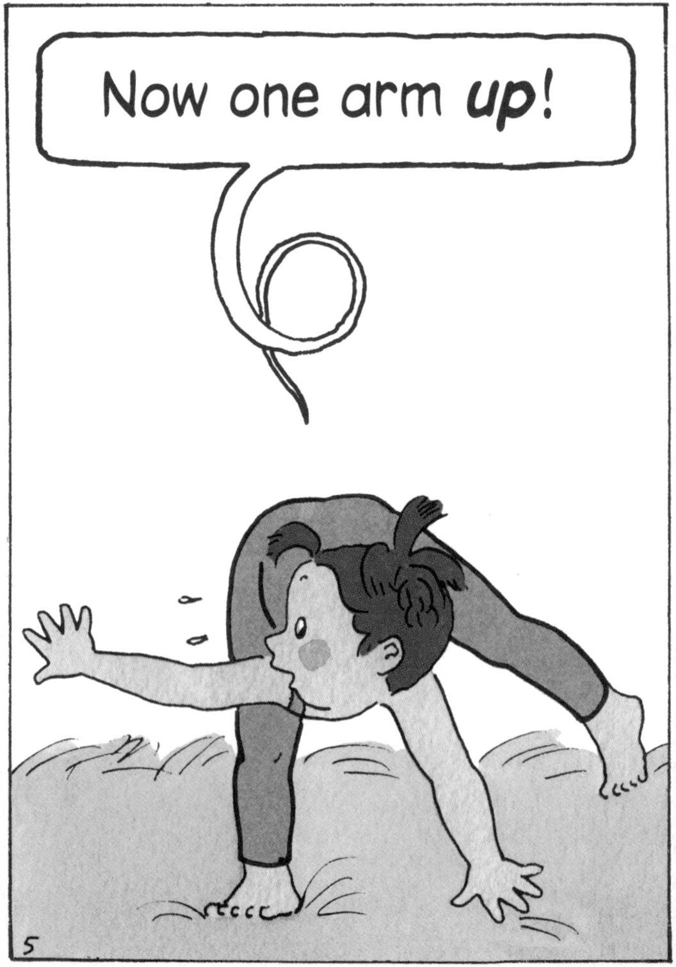
Now one arm *up*!

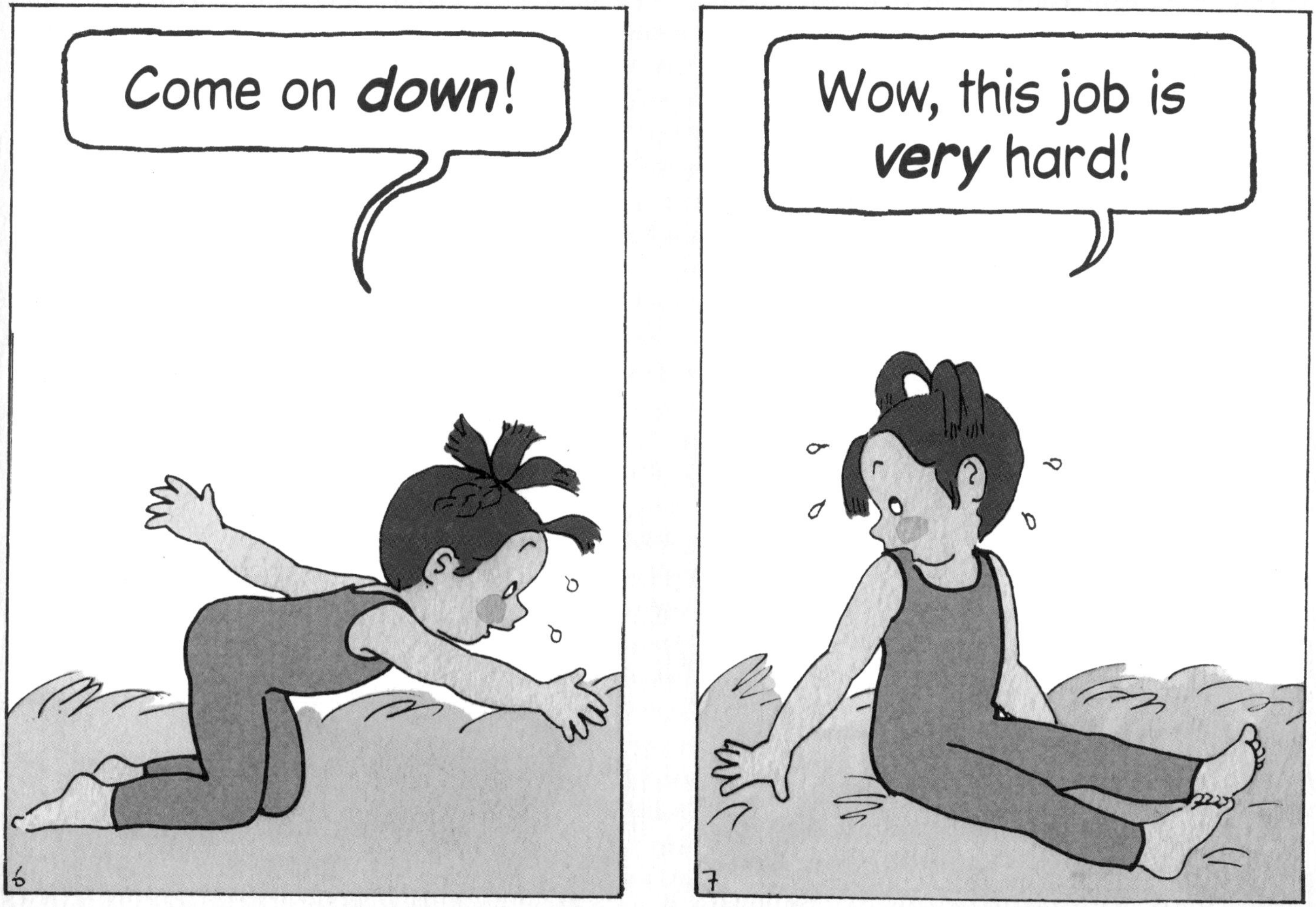
Come on **down**!
Wow, this job is **very** hard!

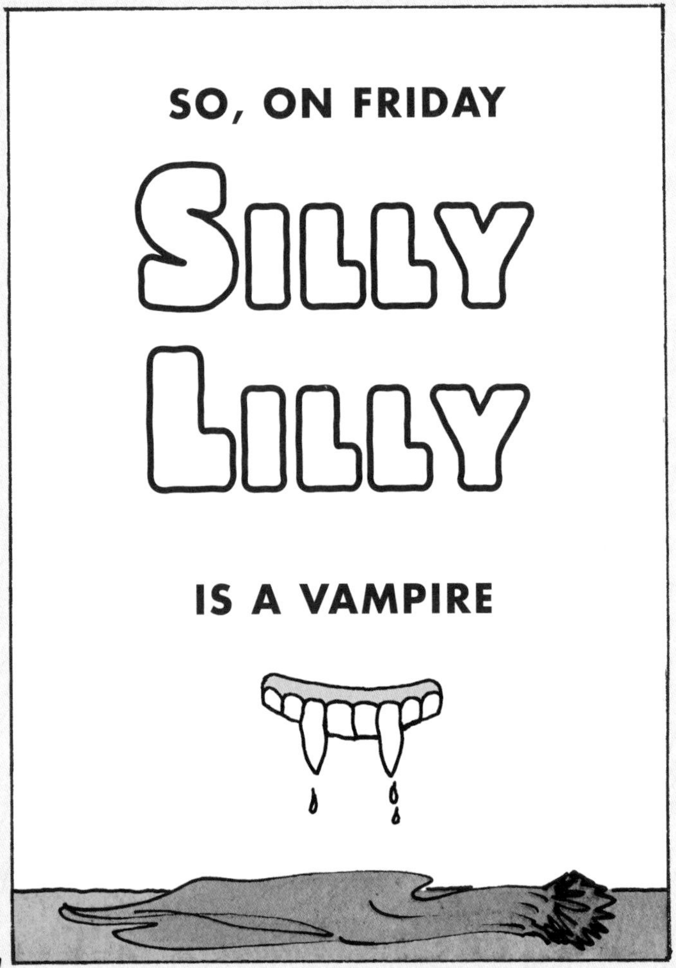
SO, ON FRIDAY
SILLY LILLY
IS A VAMPIRE

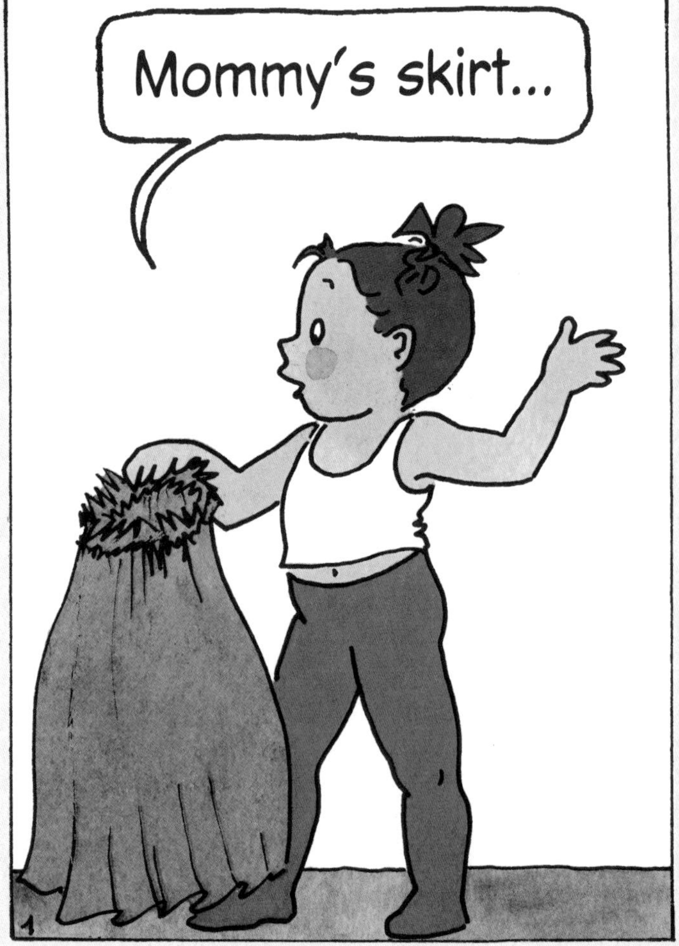
Mommy's skirt...

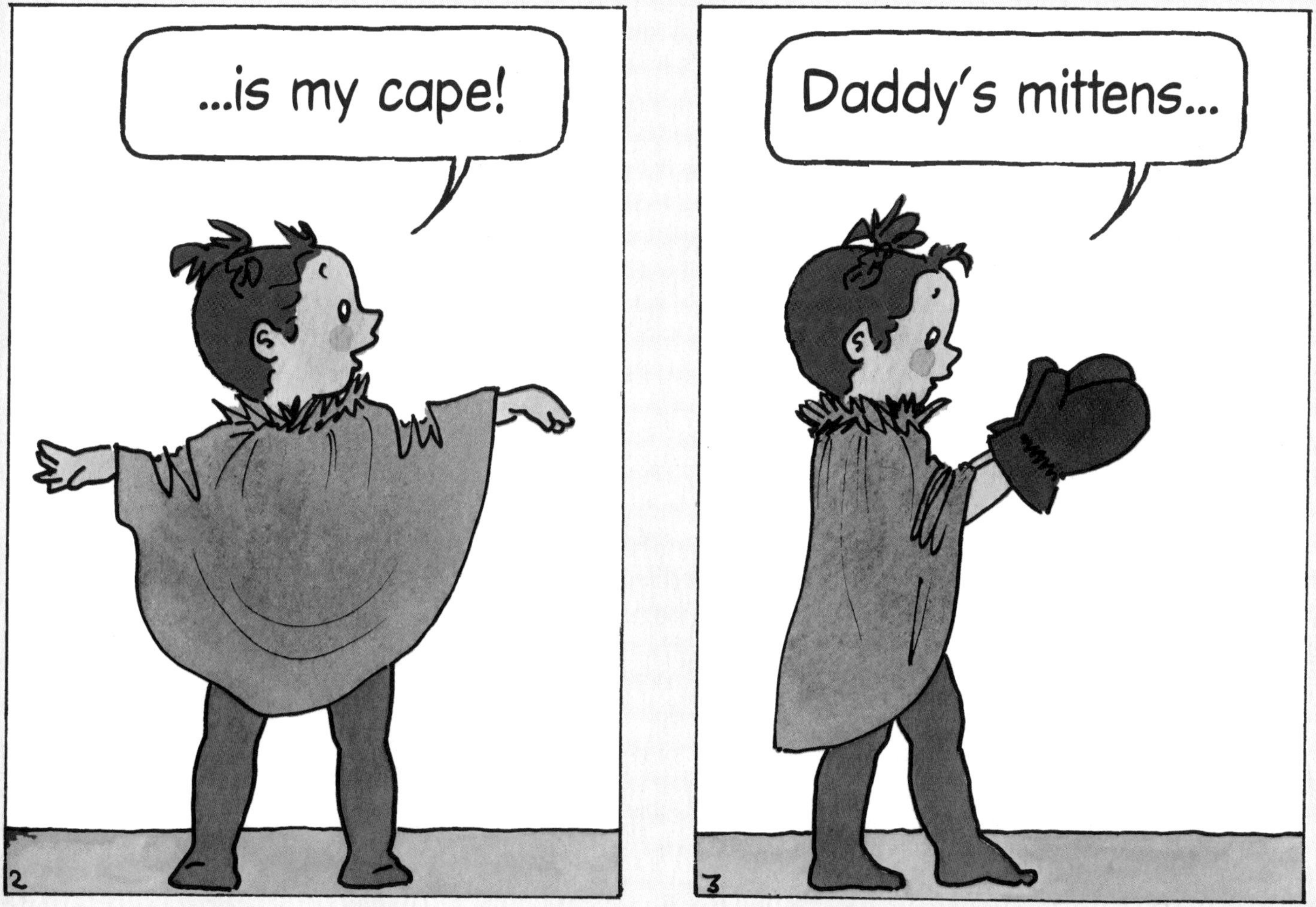
...is my cape!
Daddy's mittens...

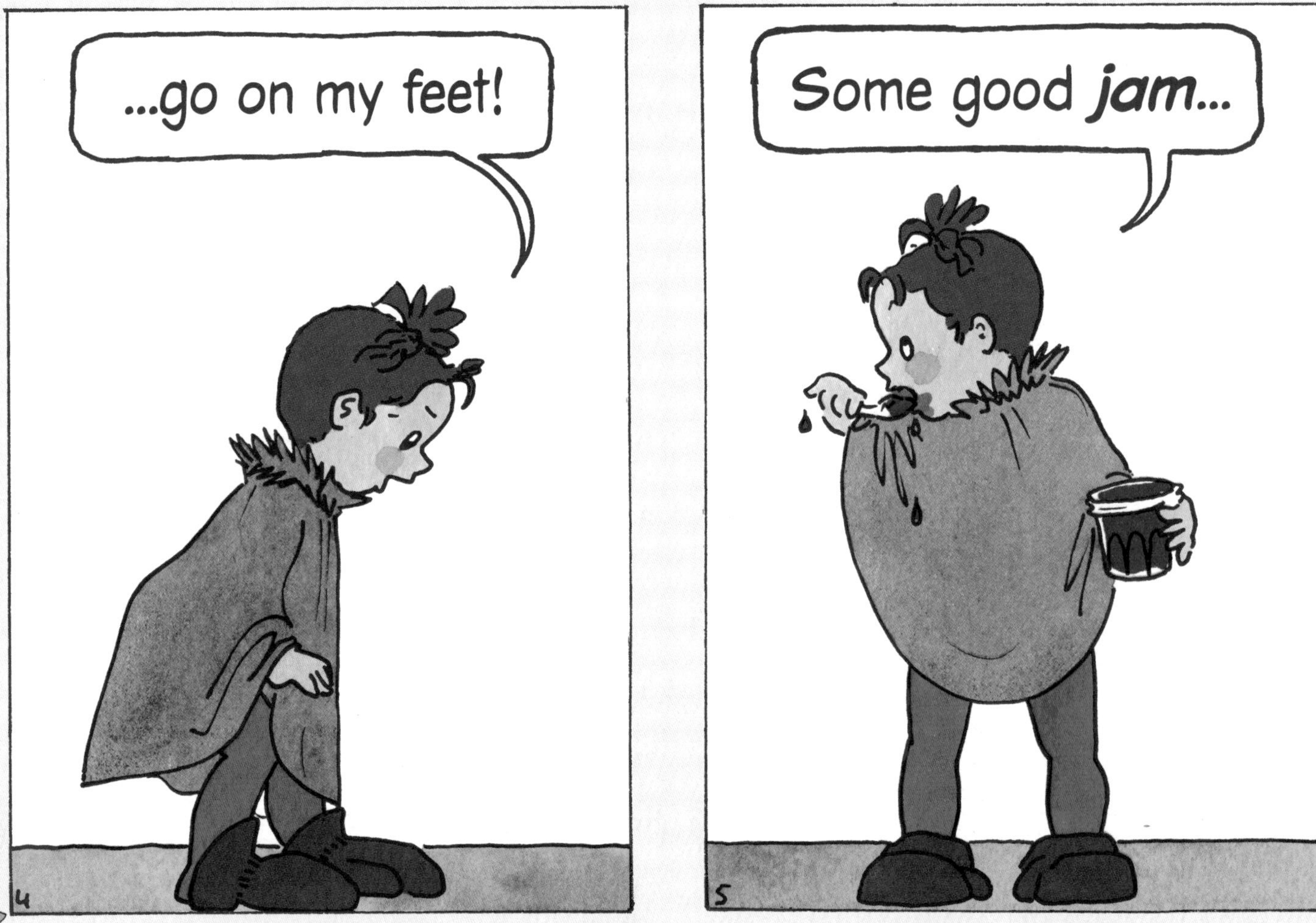
...go on my feet!
Some good *jam*...

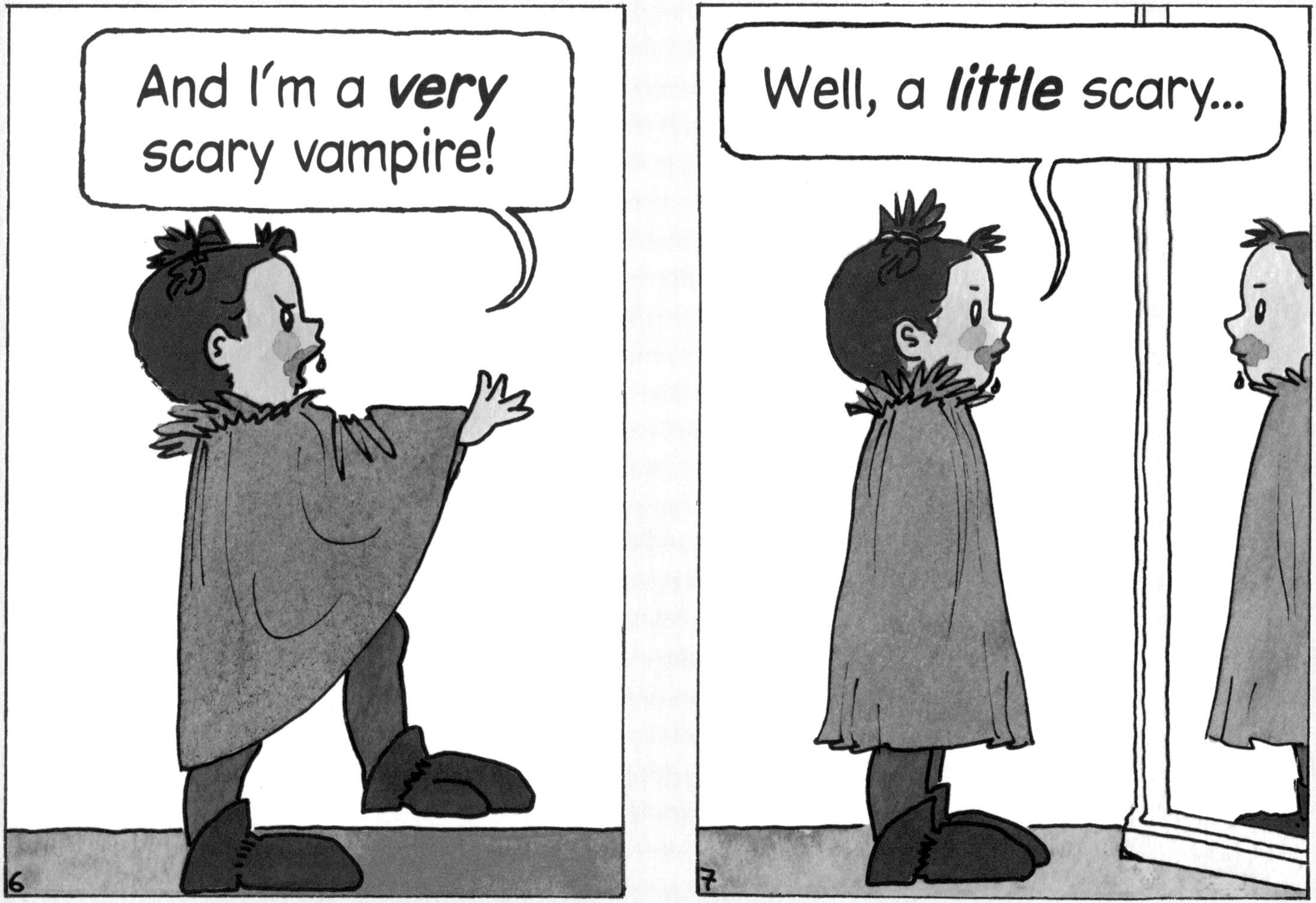
And I'm a ***very*** scary vampire!
Well, a ***little*** scary...

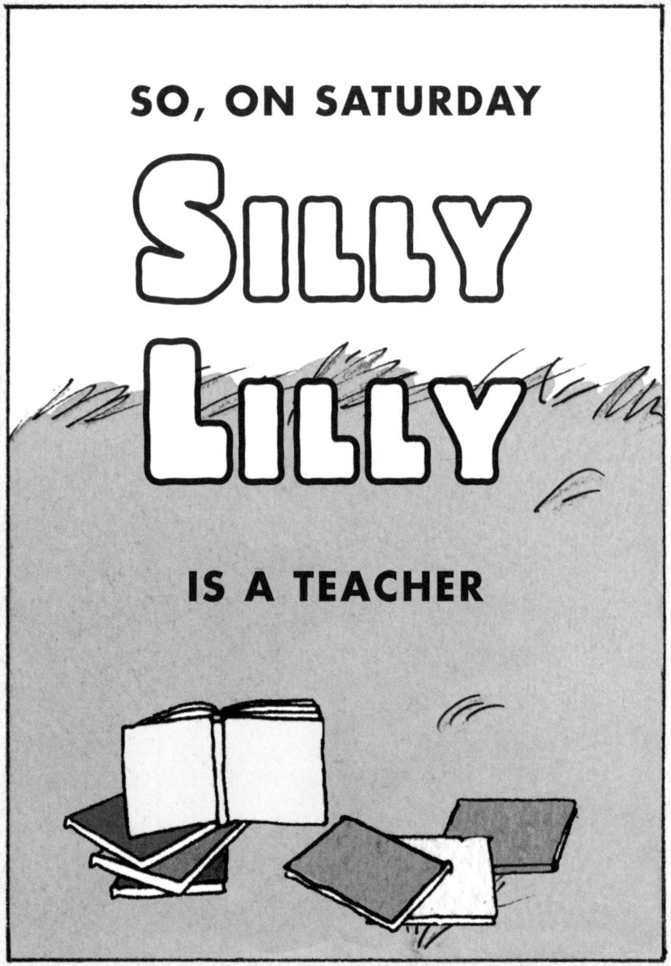
SO, ON SATURDAY
SILLY
LILLY
IS A TEACHER

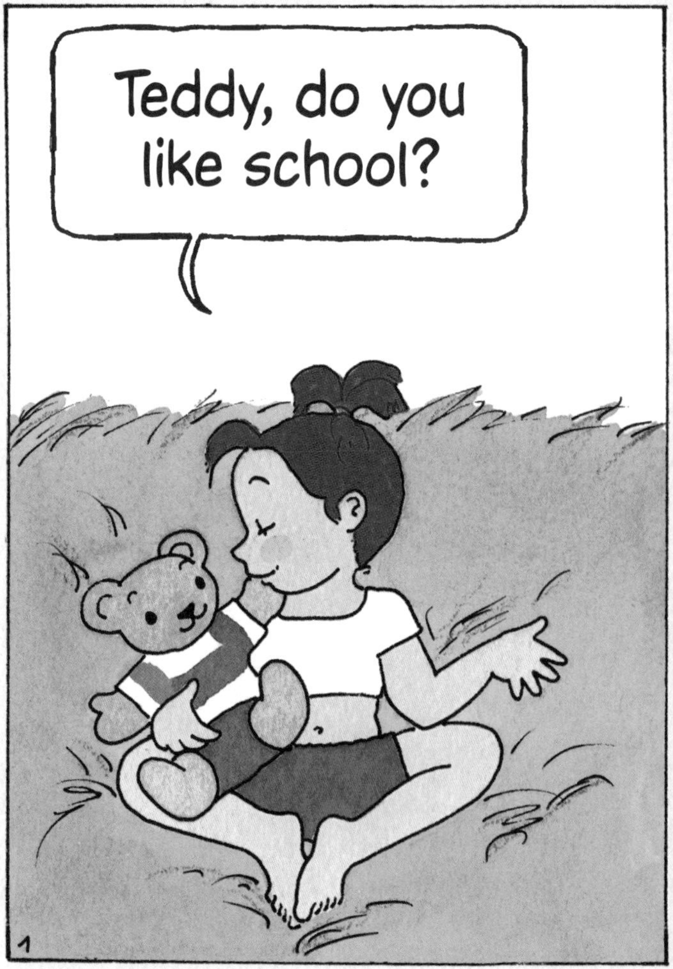
Teddy, do you like school?

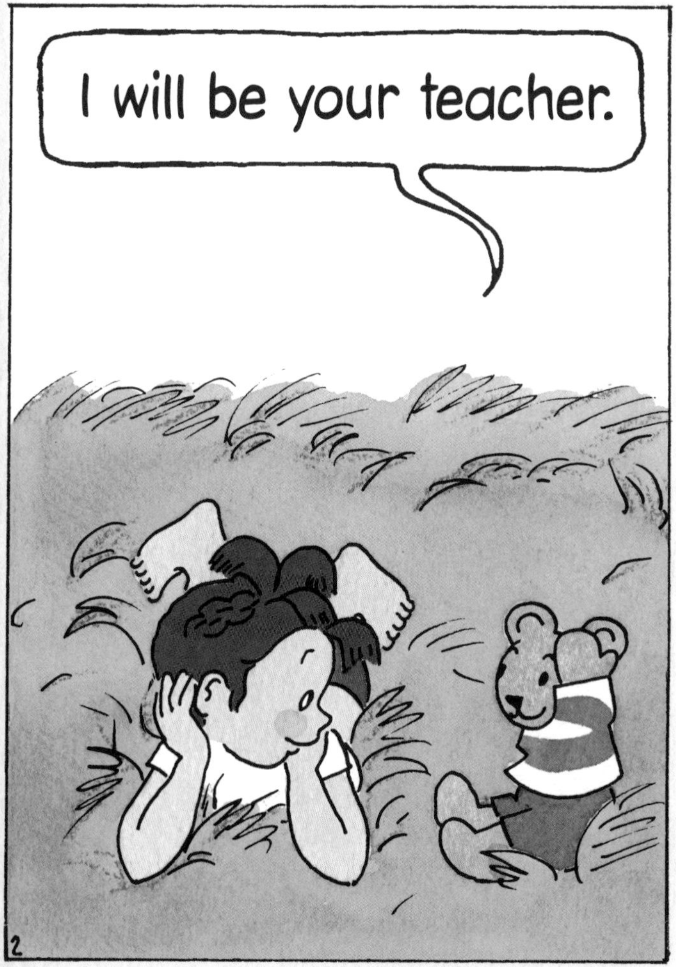
I will be your teacher.
2

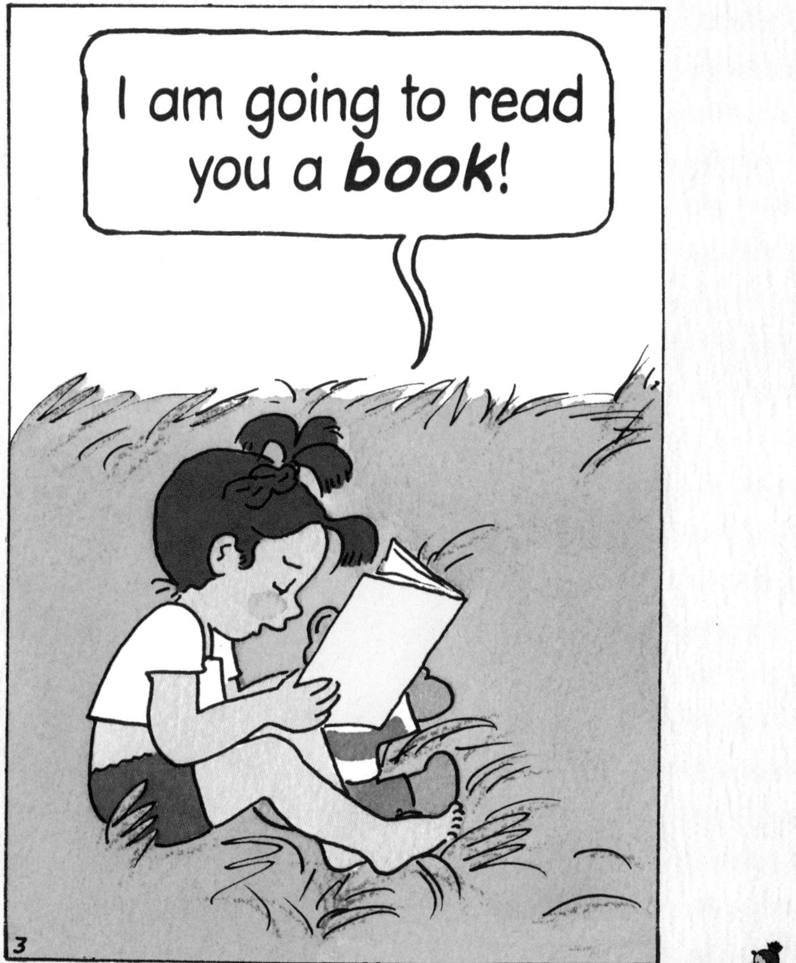
I am going to read you a **book**!
3

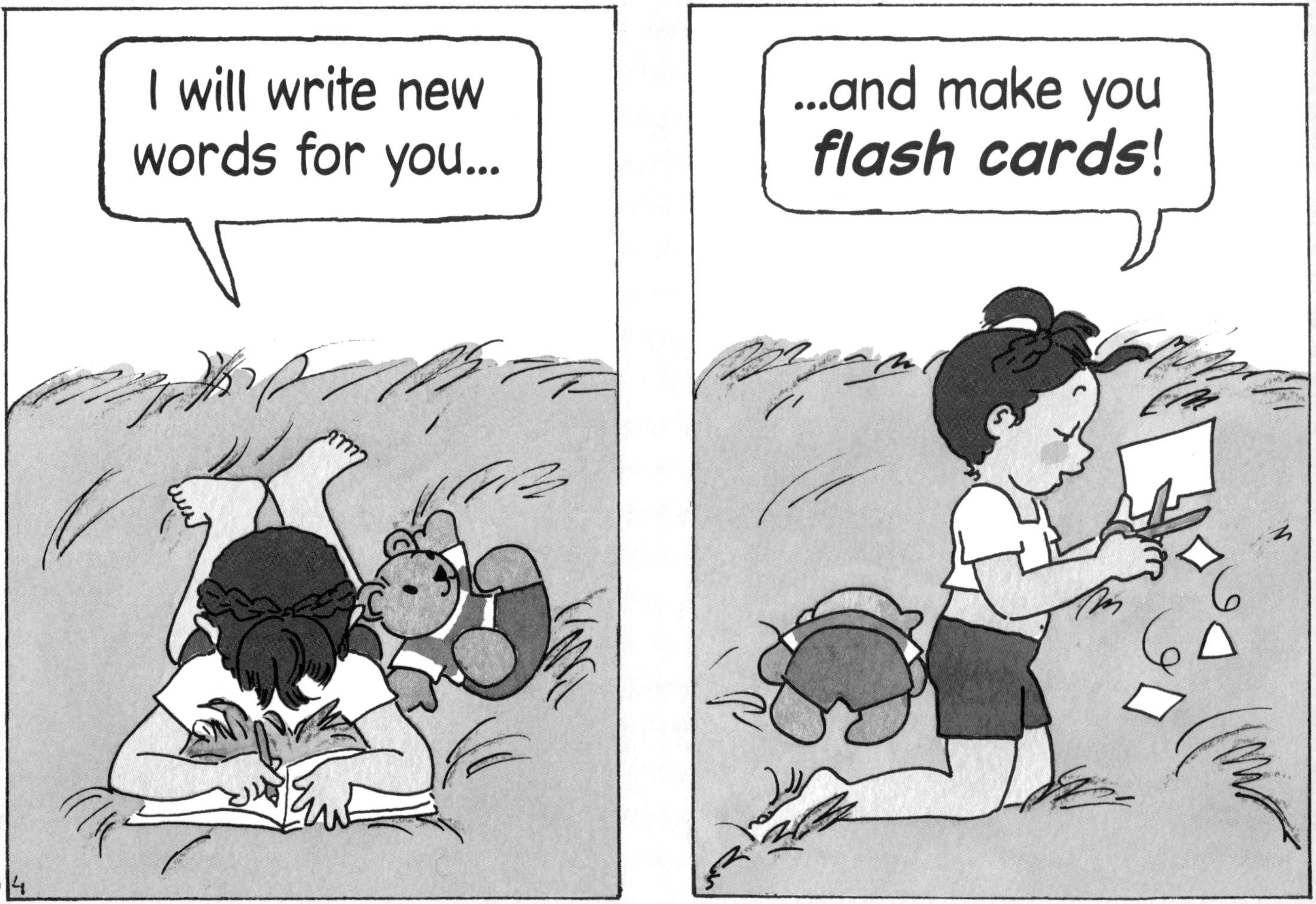
I will write new words for you...
...and make you *flash cards*!

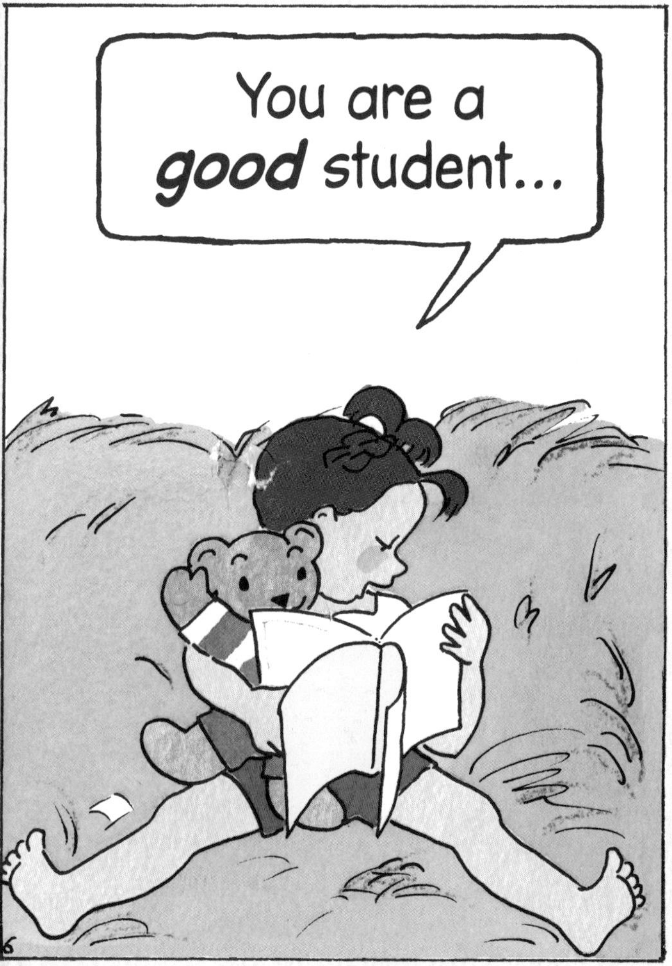
You are a *good* student...

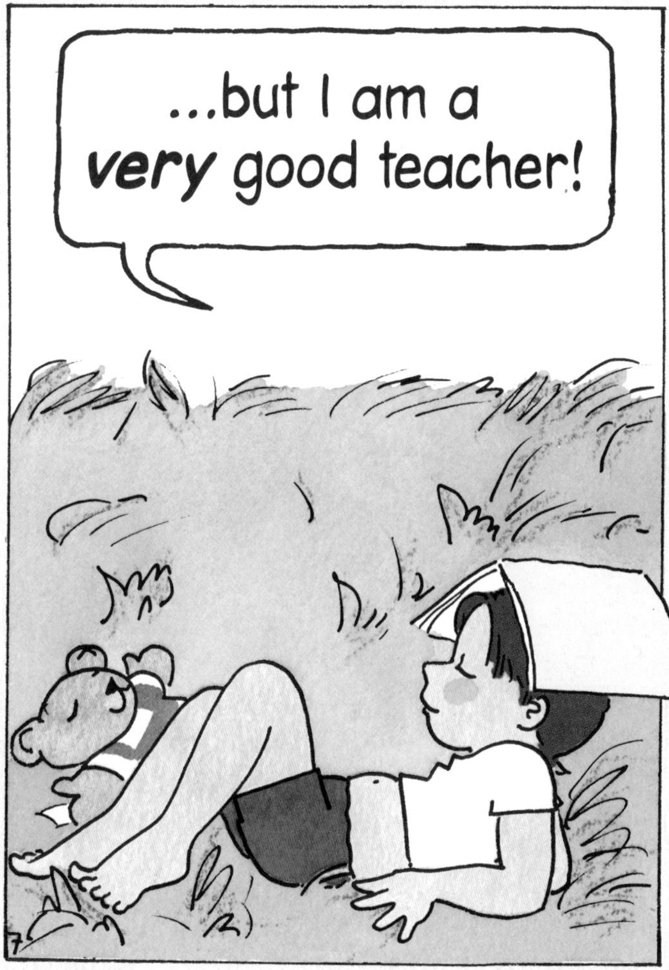
...but I am a *very* good teacher!

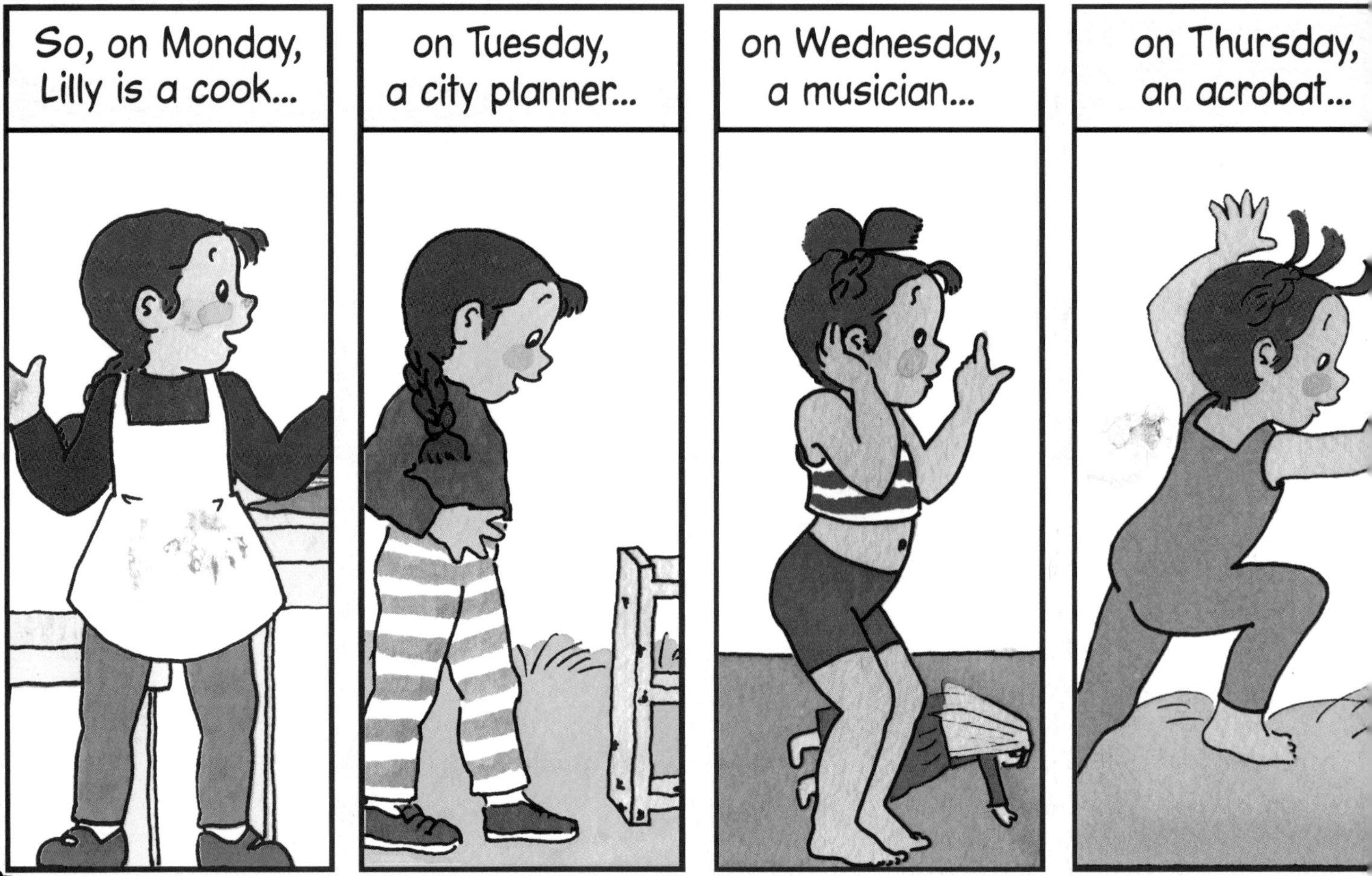
So, on Monday, Lilly is a cook...
on Tuesday, a city planner...
on Wednesday, a musician...
on Thursday, an acrobat...

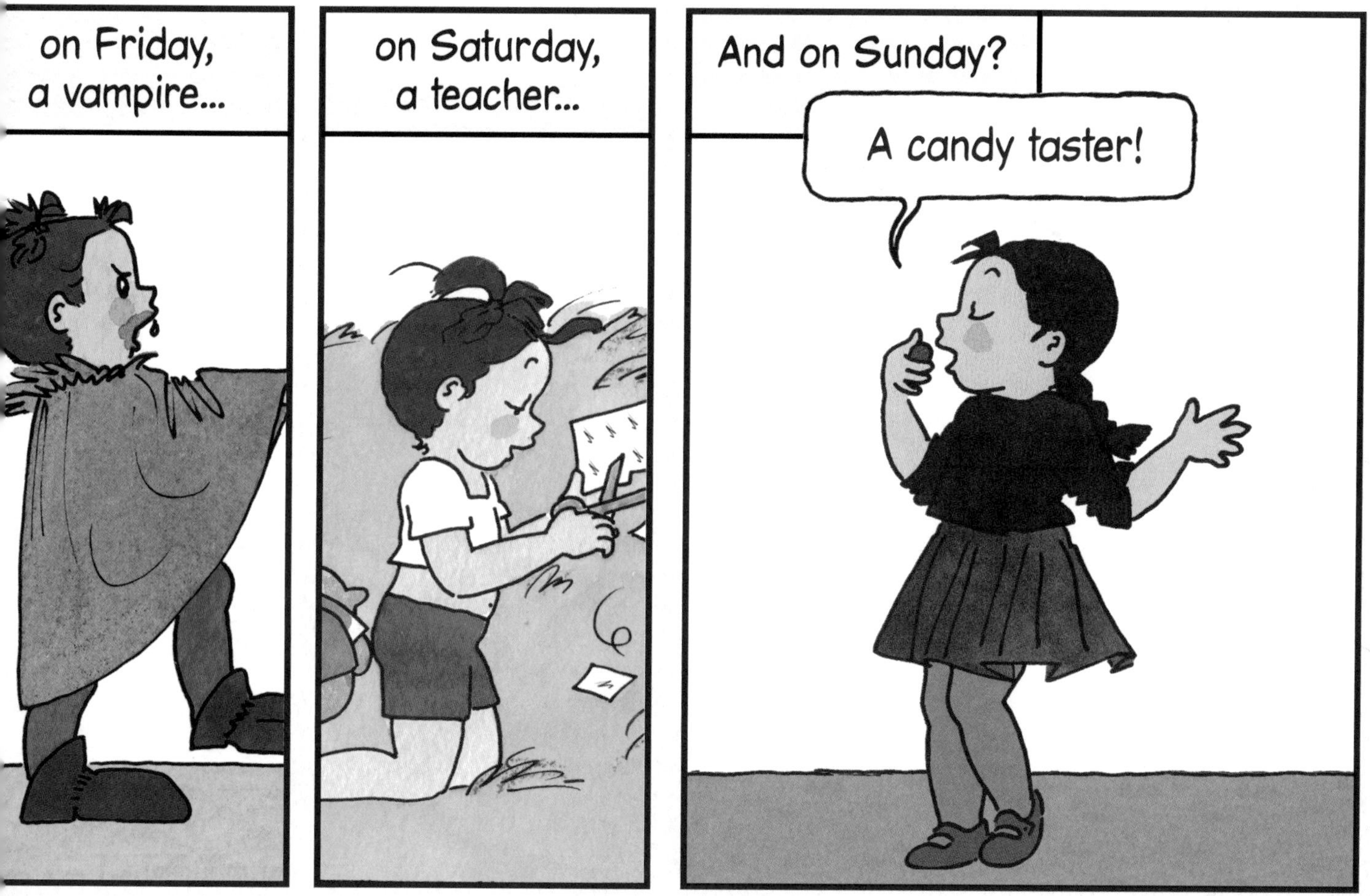
on Friday,
a vampire...
on Saturday,
a teacher...
And on Sunday?
A candy taster!

ABOUT THE AUTHOR

And what about *you*? What will *you* be?

Agnès Rosenstiehl is the beloved writer and artist of nearly a hundred children's books, many featuring the deceptively simple antics of "Mimi Cracra," Silly Lilly's French alter ego. About her first TOON Book, *Silly Lilly and the Four Seasons*, the well-known historian and critic Leonard Marcus said, in a starred review in *Publishers Weekly*: "[The] comic moments . . . that Rosenstiehl extracts from her rigorously pared-down materials draw us directly into Lilly's emotional world, where attention is routinely paid to everything, from a lowly dandelion on up. To know Lilly is to want to know what she has to say."

In 1995, Agnès Rosenstiehl received the prestigious Grand Prize for Children's Books from the Société des Gens de Lettres. Agnès is a scholar of literature as well as music, and is married to an eminent mathematician. She lives in a country house with a garden, hidden in the center of Paris. She has four children and fifteen grandchildren.

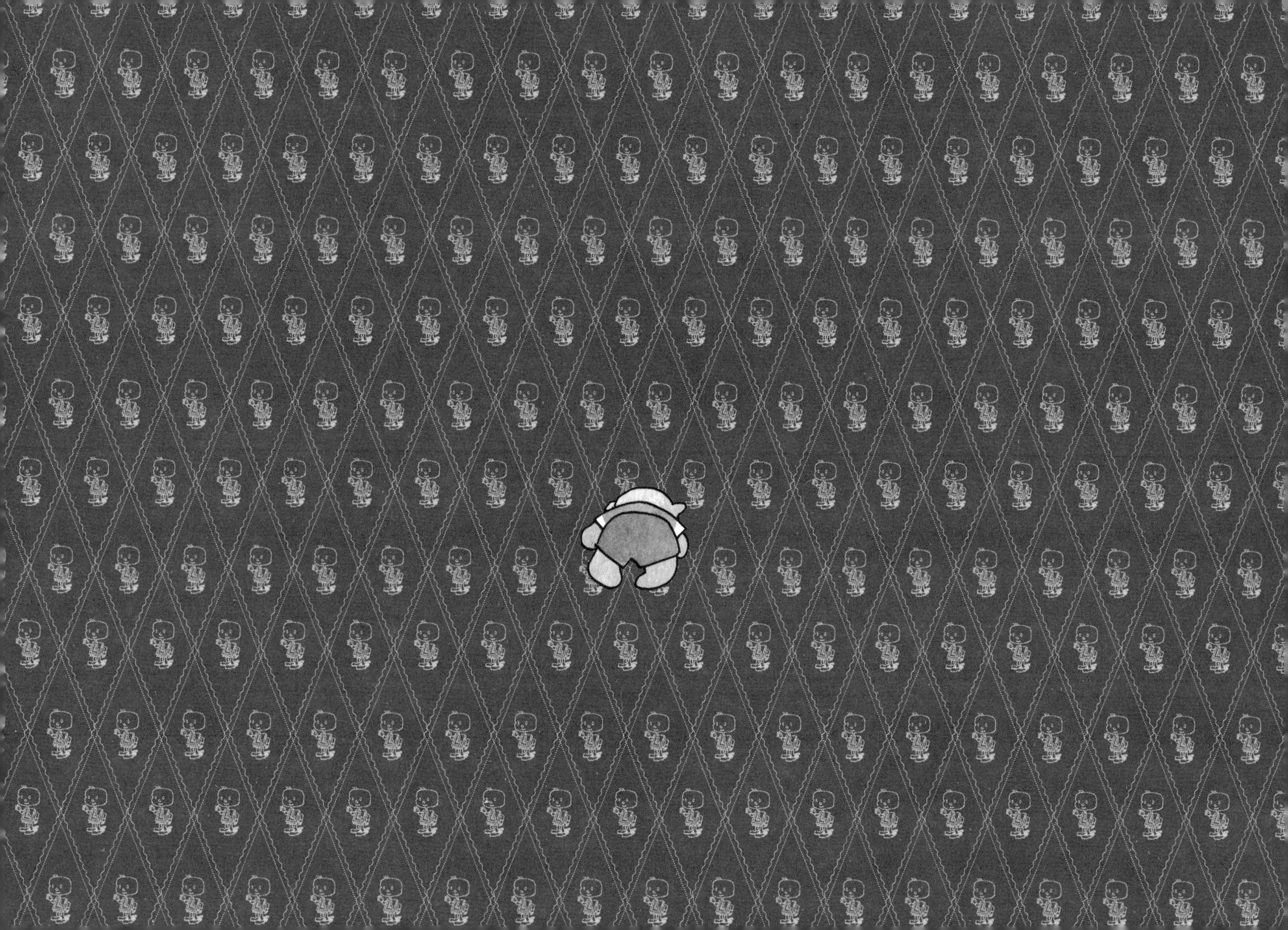

TOON INTO FUN at TOON-BOOKS.COM

TOON READERS are a revolutionary, free online tool that allows all readers to **TOON INTO READING!**

TOON READERS: you will love hearing the authors narrate their books when you click the balloons. TOON READERS are also offered in Spanish, French, Russian, Chinese and other languages, a breakthrough for all readers including English Language Learners.

Young readers are young writers: our **CARTOON MAKER** lets you create your own cartoons with your favorite TOON characters.

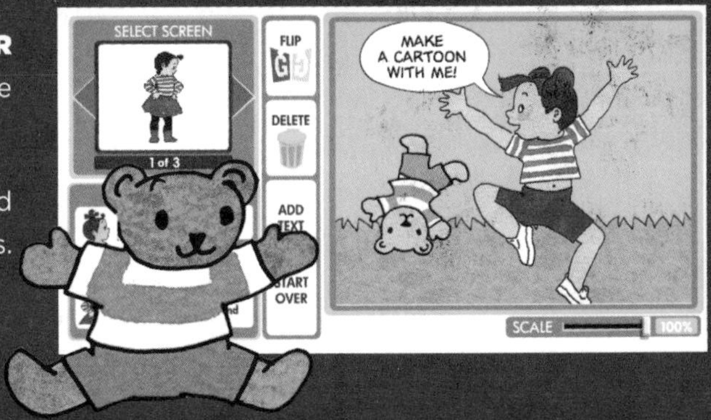
SELECT SCREEN
1 of 3
FLIP
DELETE
OVER
MAKE A CARTOON WITH ME!
SCALE
100%

And tune into our **KIDS' CARTOON GALLERY**: Send us your cartoons and come read your friends' cartoons. We post the funniest ones online for everyone to see!

Look for TOON Books on the iPhone and iPad!